A FAMILY OF TIME:
A Space Exploration Science Fiction Novel

Robert E. Murchison

Cover design by Vila Design

Published by Van Rye Publishing, LLC
Ann Arbor, MI
www.vanryepublishing.com

ISBN: 979-8-9851099-6-2 (paperback)
ISBN: 979-8-9851099-7-9 (ebook)
Library of Congress Control Number: 2022930103

Dedication

I DEDICATE THIS BOOK in memory of my wife, Denise. It was her wish that I complete it before she passed, but that didn't happen. She supported me not only in this endeavor but in everything we did during our thirty-seven-plus years of marriage. The book is also dedicated to other family members who passed after I started writing it and to my family members who are still alive today at the time of this writing.

This book is additionally dedicated to those who had the vision of space travel, to those who worked to make space travel an actuality, and to those whose lives were lost for the pursuit of space exploration. Our remembrance of people who were involved in space exploration is one key to our continued pursuit of a future in space. The names of these people would make quite a list—too long to include here, though some are mentioned in the Acknowledgments section toward the end of this book. Some made the history books, some became famous, but many of them are known only to their families and friends. As long as we continue to move forward with space exploration, the list will continue to grow.

Contents

Chapter 1

The Invitation

I T WAS A FINE late spring afternoon when Robert Mac-Murchaid decided to take a break from mowing his yard and cool off since temperatures were warmer earlier than usual in the year. He turned off the mower and headed to his front porch to relax. He poured himself a glass of tea from a pitcher on the table and sat on the porch swing to admire the view. Robert could see Poteau Mountain, where the Heavener Runestone stood as it had for centuries. He wondered, as he often did, if we would ever find proof other than the runestones (Heavener, Poteau, Shawnee, and others) that the Vikings had made it that far west.

In Robert's mind, he could see the runestone—a Savannah sandstone monolith once called "Indian Rock." He visualized the eight runes etched into its face by pre-Columbian Norsemen. To him, it did not matter if the runes were interpreted as reading November 11, 1012, or Glome Dal (Glome's Valley). What mattered to him was that a man made his permanent mark in time. Oral traditions indicated that there was a cave somewhere that might hold more information about the people who had carved the runes. But no such cave had yet been found. Robert wondered if it might happen during his lifetime.

Robert's thoughts were interrupted when a car with government plates pulled into his driveway. He got up to see who it was and why a government official would be visiting his home. Though he was used to seeing government vehicles around the area and during his former time in the United States Air Force, one had never stopped directly at his house before. To his surprise, it was US Congressman Geoff Pitts who got out of the vehicle. "Hello, Robert," Geoff said. "How are you and your family doing these days?"

"We're doing okay. Denise is visiting her folks, and the kids are down the street with their friends. Come grab a seat. Would you like some tea?" Robert hadn't seen Geoff in years and was understandably curious as to why he had come to Heavener, Oklahoma. Geoff rarely left DC, and when he did, he usually headed to his hometown of Muskogee. "Did Capitol Hill get tired of you and kick you out?"

"Heck no! It would take more than an act of congress for them to get rid of me," Geoff quipped. "Yes, that tea looks mighty refreshing."

The two men sat and chatted a while about friends, family, and old times. Geoff, who had been staring at Poteau Mountain for some time himself, turned to Robert and said, "You know, I've been meaning to take a close look-see at that slab of stone up yonder. You wanna tag along?"

Surprised, Robert responded, "Yes." He knew that something unusual was up because Geoff usually more formally referred to the runestone as a marker in time and hardly ever used that many slang words in one sentence. *Geoff must have something important he needs to talk to me about*, Robert thought. "Let me leave a note so the family will know where I am, and I'll lock up the house."

Hardly a word was said as the men headed across town to the Heavener Runestone state park and up the road to the parking area. Once they arrived, they headed directly to the building housing the twelve-foot-high sandstone slab. While admiring the runestone, Geoff finally revealed the real reason behind his visit. "The reason I'm here is to offer you and your family a special invitation."

As Robert looked on, intrigued, the congressman continued. "Since I'm on the financial committee for Universal Space Agency funding, I get to see almost every project before it's approved or rejected. You and your son, Kris, have submitted some interesting ideas to us during the past few years. One of those ideas we're planning to implement in the near future. The United States has sent men, women, couples, and representatives of different ethnic groups into space but has yet to send an entire family. In the coming weeks, we'll be making an official announcement that within the next year, we'll send an entire family to the International Space Station. And we'll credit Kris and you for this idea."

Robert could not help but smile. He thought about the information he and his wife, Denise, had managed to gather to help Kris and his teammates for their science fair. He also thought about how his family had watched most of the shuttle launches on television and watched videos about the history of manned space flight, all of which led to him and Kris submitting several ideas to the Universal Space Agency over the years.

What Geoff said next almost knocked Robert to his knees. "We want *your* family to be the family we send. What do you say?"

Robert stood there, unsure what to say or if he would be able to speak at all. He thought to himself, *Denise will wake me up any second now, and all of this will have been a dream.* But in reality, he knew, *This is no dream!*

"Are you okay, Robert?" Geoff asked. "Earth to Robert! Come on, snap out of it. I realize this must be a shock, but the runes are showing more life than you, my friend."

After gathering himself, Robert finally responded, "I'm okay, but I'm not sure I heard you correctly. *My* family is to be that family?!"

"You heard me right, Robert. We want you, Denise, and the kids on a flight to the space station within the next year. We realize none of you have the years of training astronauts go through, but we'll give you a crash course. For now, you must keep all of this completely secret from everyone. And I know from your military background working with the Titan II Intercontinental Ballistic Missile that you understand me fully on that. We want to build this event up as much as possible. Even the president hasn't been informed yet as to which family we've selected."

Robert pondered everything for a minute and then asked, "Are Denise and the kids to know, or am I to keep them in the dark as well? And what about my extended family since we cannot simply take off and stay away for such a long time without explanation?"

"We'll inform Denise and your children once we're airborne on the way to Florida for your training. I have a cover story that will satisfy everyone as to why I'm here and why we're going to Florida. The story is that I'm taking you and your family on a vacation that I personally promised you some time ago. That's what we'll go with until Denise's parents and your parents are picked up to meet us at the Universal Space Center in Florida."

Robert suspected there was more that Geoff wasn't revealing. But for the time being, he didn't push the issue. As Robert and Geoff walked around the park some more, Robert shared some of the history he knew about different spots in the park. Eventually, they headed back to Geoff's vehicle and back to Robert's house. When they arrived there, it seemed like everyone and their cat was there and waiting.

Denise, who had returned home, immediately greeted the men at the car. "I came home to a note stating that you would be back shortly, and all the neighbors are asking me what a government vehicle was doing here." At that moment, she noticed Geoff getting out of the driver's side of the car. "Oh! Hi, Geoff," Denise said, smiling and changing her tone. "What brings you to our neck of the woods?" She no longer seemed worried, but her curiosity was now peaked. Meanwhile, Nicole and Troy-Cook sat on the MacMurchaids' porch swing, trying to contain their curiosity while pretending to be little angels.

"Let's all go inside, honey . . . and kids," Robert suggested. "We'll explain everything in there." Robert ushered Denise,

Nicole, and Troy-Cook inside while Geoff followed. "Okay, where are Kris and Tony?"

"At the DEAR pen, Dad," Nicole said with a smirk on her face.

Robert understood her play on words about the deer pen, but he pretended not to notice. Then, he asked Troy-Cook, "Will you please go get your brothers? Hurry but watch the traffic."

Troy was already halfway out the door and grabbing his bike when he answered his dad with, "Yes, sir!" Within ten minutes, he was back, followed by his brothers.

"Get your butts in here, you Casanovas," Robert said teasingly. "And close the door." Once everyone was seated, he began by asking his family a question. "When was the last time this family had a real vacation?"

Denise answered jokingly, "We haven't. We've been too broke for that."

Tony added his two cent's worth, "A vacation? Huh?! What's *that*?"

"Exactly!" Troy chimed in as he pointed at Tony.

"Well, would you like to go to Florida on vacation?"

Geoff had barely finished the question when the kids all yelled, "YES!"

"When are we going? When are we going?" Nicole pleaded.

Denise, with an inquisitive and puzzled look on her face, asked, "What's the catch?"

Geoff responded, "No catch. I promised Robert a while back that I would take your family on vacation, and I'm simply making good on that promise. I've made arrangements for you to visit the Universal Space Center and a few attractions while we're in Florida."

"Like I asked, what's the catch?" Denise asked again, still puzzled. She glanced with a raised eyebrow back and forth between Robert and Geoff while she waited for an answer.

Before either man could answer, Troy blurted out, "Come on, Mom, let's just go! Dad wouldn't even have this discussion if he didn't think it was all right! Come on, please? *Please?!* *Pretty* Please?!" He and the rest of the children went into their sad puppy-dog routine.

Denise, trying not to laugh, yelled, "Okay! Okay! I give up! We'll go. Now stop." With that, the kids gave each other high fives.

Geoff told Denise, "I'll go into more detail once we're airborne. For now, don't you think you should start getting things together for your vacation?"

"Well, that will be a limited number of things since we can't be away from home *too* long," Denise answered. "And what will we do about the animals, Robert?"

"And Dad, what about—" Kris began to ask but was interrupted by his father.

"Don't worry; Geoff has covered all the bases and taken care of all the details," Robert reassured everyone. "Let's get ready because our ride to the plane will be here shortly."

Chapter 2

A Flight of Surprises

THE MACMURCHAIDS and Congressman Pitts arrived at Fort Smith Municipal Airport. Their vehicle did not head to the terminal but instead to the Arkansas Air National Guard side of the airport, where their flight would be on a US Air Force C-130 Hercules personnel carrier. They exited the vehicle and entered the plane through a side door. Robert noticed that this "Hurky Bird" (as he grew up knowing it) had been modified. The space that was normally used for carrying troops had been divided into rooms.

Geoff led the family through a doorway into the aircraft and said, "Come on in. We need to get seated and buckled in. We'll be taking off shortly." Just as he finished his statement, the engines started, and their roar, even though somewhat muffled, was all the passengers could hear for a while.

Once everyone was inside and seated, Geoff closed the doors and pulled a heavy curtain across them. All was quiet. "We've soundproofed these rooms and mounted them on a suspension system, which suppresses most of the vibrations felt during flight," Geoff informed the passengers. "Most of what you see here and in the adjoining rooms has been developed for the Universal Space Agency and the military by private contractors. I'll give you a tour once we get to cruising altitude. Until then, please relax but be ready to buckle up if needed."

After each of them was seated, they were automatically buckled in. "Don't be alarmed," Geoff reassured them. "That's just the automatic safety system at work. Once we reach our cruising altitude, your belts will unlock and allow you to get up and move about."

Troy asked, "When are we going to take off?" But as he spoke, everyone's buckles automatically released. "Never mind," he said. They were already up in the air. It was so smooth that Troy hadn't even noticed.

Geoff got up and said, "I promised a tour. So, who's ready?"

The kids all said at once, "Me!"

Before Geoff could start the tour, Robert asked him, "Wasn't there something we were supposed to do once we were airborne?"

"That can wait until after the tour, Robert. Come on, everyone." Geoff waived for them to follow him.

The MacMurchaids proceeded into the next room. It contained a small dining area on one side, and on the other side, there were chairs with consoles in front of them and controls on the chairs' arms. "This is our dining slash rec room," Geoff informed everyone. "We have plenty of food and drinks at that counter. And these," Geoff said, pointing toward the chairs and consoles, "are video centers. You can watch videos and play games at them. You insert discs into the readers in the side of the consoles and use the controls on the arms of the chairs. The centers can be operated individually or tied in together. The images use three-dimensional viewing, except that it's an updated version that doesn't require 3D glasses."

"Can we try now, please?!" Troy pleaded with Robert.

"Maybe later," Geoff jumped in. "I still have more to show you." With that, Geoff led the group into the next room. They entered what appeared to be a divided locker room. "This is where we can change clothes if need be. And if nature calls, we have one toilet for women and one for men. We also have a shower stall on each side. If the ladies will head to this side and the guys to the other, I would like you to check out the lockers." The family members headed to their perspective sides.

"Hey! This locker has my name on it!" Troy said with a puzzled look on his face.

"Yes," Geoff responded. "You each have a locker with your name on it. If you open them and look inside, you'll find something else interesting, too." Each family member opened their locker to find clothes and shoes inside. As they took the clothes out, each of them noticed that the clothes were similar to the *Star Trek®* original series uniforms but slightly different. The uniforms had a modified Universal Space Agency emblem on one side and their name on the other. "We knew your family enjoyed all the *Star Trek®* television series and movies, so we had these uniforms made for you. They're not exact Federation uniforms since we do not have permission for that. But . . . go ahead and try them on!"

The family members separated and changed into their uniforms and shoes. Then, they returned to see how everyone looked. Kris gave the Vulcan hand salute and said, "Live long and prosper."

Tony responded, "Since you took what I was going to say, I'll just say good luck." And he returned the hand gesture.

"Well, how do they fit?" Geoff asked everyone. Everyone responded that the uniforms and shoes fit perfectly. "A little birdie told me your sizes," Geoff said with a wink. "Since they fit, you can follow me back to the lounge so that I can take care of the 'business' Robert hinted at before the tour." Once everyone was seated again, Geoff handed a disc to Robert. "Please insert it into the large video console. Then, type Bravo-Delta-One/Vid-One and hit enter."

After Robert did as instructed, the presidential seal appeared on the console screen. Then, the president himself appeared. He said, "I want to take this opportunity to congratulate you for being chosen to be a part of our next step in space exploration—the first family in space."

Denise exclaimed, "What?!" Geoff and Robert both put fingers to their lips and shushed her.

The video continued with the president saying, "Though I don't yet know who you are, Congressman Pitts assures me that you were carefully selected because of your diverse but unifying traits. Within a year, you'll launch with one of our crews, heading to the International Space Station aboard one of our newest spacecrafts. It's my understanding that this mission has been given the name 'Valhalla' by Congressman Pitts. He told me about one of the translations of the runes on the Heavener Runestone near you and how the stone itself is a marker in time to be shared with all people.

"This mission is much like the runestone in that it will be shared by all the people of Earth," the president continued. "You'll be representing not only the United States but the whole planet as a family. I understand that Valhalla is the Vikings' version of heaven. Since you'll be flying into the heavens, it is only fitting to say you're flying to Valhalla. I'm looking forward to meeting you at the press conference later. Until then, I wish you good luck, and I send my heartfelt congratulations." The presidential seal reappeared, and then the console's screen went blank.

"Vacation, huh?" Denise remarked with a look that could kill an entire army. "I knew there had to be a catch. And just what gives you the right to shush me anyhow?" She stood with her knuckles on her hips. "I want answers, like . . . last week. And you . . ." she said, looking at Robert, "I want to know how long you've known about all of this."

"Before I let Robert get hung out to dry," Geoff interjected, "he only knew part of it. I haven't even told the president everything yet." Geoff then turned to Robert. "Robert, please enter Glome's-Valhalla/Bravo-Delta-Two/Gamma-Victor-One/Decode/Display." When Robert did so, the large console screen came alive again but generated a CGI display. "This is what we have planned for your family's mission." Geoff pointed to the outlined images and explained the plan for the MacMurchaids' mission to the International Space Station.

"One: We send you up in our newest spacecraft to be in Earth orbit for one day.

"Two: On day two, the craft will maneuver into position to

dock with the International Space Station.

"Three: You'll spend two to three weeks on the station doing various activities while we record you.

"Four: While you're there, your bodies will be adjusted to a one-sixth gravitational force, generated in a specially-modified section of the station.

"Five: Once we feel you've adjusted enough, we'll have you board a special shuttle craft, which is code-named Valkyrie and was built in space for your flight to the moon."

The whole family's mouths were slightly open, and the looks on their faces were priceless to Geoff. They each wanted to ask questions but didn't dare until Geoff was finished. He continued.

"Six: Once you reach the moon, you'll head to the dark side before descending to the surface.

"Seven: Your descent will take you to a platform built within Jules Verne, which is a crater that is 3,037 miles lunar east and 750 miles lunar south of Tranquility Base where Apollo 11 landed.

"Eight: The platform will retract into a cavern discovered on the side of the crater. The cavern has been modified with tunnels and rooms added on for human occupation. We have named this facility 'Valhalla.'

"Nine: Once inside Valhalla, you'll be given a tour by technicians who we have dubbed 'angels' so that you can become acquainted with the facility and with Odin, who is the computer that operates the facility.

"Ten: The angels will then prep you for a short stay in your sleep chambers."

"Whoa! Wait one minute!" Denise said, stopping Geoff. "What do you mean 'prepped?!' And what are these sleep chambers?!" Denise inquired. Geoff hit pause on a remote control by his chair. "I'm not doing anything of the sort until I know what this all means and whether it's safe or not," Denise continued. "So, you better start explaining, or this so-called vacation is over now, and you'll turn this plane around to take us home!"

"But Mom, you can't be serious," Nicole said, going back into her sad puppy-dog routine.

"Yeah, Mom, don't let your undies get into a bundle," Tony added with a smirk on his face.

"You know what I mean, kids. And as for you, you little smart aleck . . ." Denise headed for Tony, acting as if she were going to choke him. Tony got up laughing while backing away from his mom.

"If you two would please sit back down," Geoff implored, "I would be glad to explain the sleep chambers and their purpose." Everyone headed back to their seats but not before making a few more gestures toward each other. "Now, children, if you're through, I will begin again."

The children turned toward Geoff and began acting as though they were total angels. "Don't give me that," Denise warned them, "because we all know better." Denise pooched out her bottom lip as if she were pouting, and Tony stuck his tongue out at her.

"Okay, enough of that," Geoff pleaded. "May I continue?" Everyone straightened up as Geoff continued the presentation. "The sleep chambers are a method we're using to prove that you can learn while you're in a state of hibernation. Each chamber is set up to provide the individual in it with information through a variety of sensors. The subjects each person learns will be programmed into Odin according to his or her interests plus educational needs and up-to-date world events. Most of the data inputs your bodies will receive are provided through a special helmet, similar to this one." Geoff pulled a helmet out of a box sitting next to him. The helmet appeared to be one that a fighter pilot would wear but nowhere near as bulky.

Geoff continued. "I can see by the looks on your faces that you can see it resembles what a fighter pilot wears. There are differences, though. Specialized sensors have been placed throughout the helmet to help provide input to specific areas of your brain—for example, the area for sight. If visual input is required, Odin can send digitized images to the region of the brain with central visual input from your eyes. In your mind, you'll 'see' the image as clear as if you were seeing it in person. The only sensors we have yet to duplicate are smell and taste. Since memory is an active part of those senses anyway, we have utilized memory to compensate for the lack of actual input. The full extent of what your helmets can do will be explained while you take a crash course in astronaut training.

"Now, as far as being prepped for the sleep chambers, all that entails is taking a specialized shower, putting on your T-shirts and shorts, donning your helmets, and climbing into your individualized sleep chambers. By individualized, I mean they'll be molded to each of you for maximum comfort. Once inside, the angels will hook up your helmets' sensors and close the sleep chamber canopies. I know, Denise, that you have claustrophobia. Don't worry; the canopies are made of a clear material so that you can see out, and the next step of the process will have you in hibernation within a couple of seconds anyway. Now, back to the planned schedule. Please direct your attention to the console.

"Eleven: Your chambers will be filled with Loki's Breath, which will cause your bodies to enter a state of hibernation on the verge of suspended animation. This state that your bodies will enter is something we refer to as 'pseudo-death.' Now, before you all blow another gasket, I'll explain. Loki's Breath is a specialized gas, which will basically suspend all bodily functions down to the cellular level, except for the electro-chemical activity of the brain. In other words, you'll still receive and remember sensory input via the helmet, but the gas will also supply the basic needs your brains require to survive and function. We named the gas Loki's Breath since Loki was a Norse god known for mischief, and he loved to play tricks on humans and the other gods.

"The reason we call the state of hibernation you'll be in pseudo-death is that, since your bodily functions down to the cellular level will basically cease—except for the aforementioned brain activity—the body is as close to death as it can be without actually dying. But it's perfectly safe! We've been using the gas at one of our research labs for the past five years with a 99.995 percent success rate. That .005 percent failure rate was due to a test subject having a parasite in the brain that we didn't know about. The parasite was determined to be the actual cause of death. And we have since developed a way to detect this parasite and have not had any more failures. There-fore, if you subtract the death due to the parasite, Loki's Breath is 100 percent safe. Even I was a test subject for a few days. The gas has enough mixture of oxygen in it to meet your body's needs at such a slow metabolism.

"And there's more. In the subjects evaluated under Loki's Breath, we found that they neither aged nor deteriorated while under. In fact, it seems that their health was minutely *improved* over the short exposure of a few months. We're still doing studies on this beneficial side-effect with longer durations of exposure. For now, anyone awakening from pseudo-death will be at full functioning capacity within a couple of minutes. It has been described by our test subjects as waking up from a good night's sleep, except for the increased knowledge gained during their 'sleep.' Now, let's continue.

"Twelve: The angels will check that everything is function-ing properly. Once this is assured, they'll enter the craft that took you to the moon, and it will exit your Valhalla facility. Once the facility is secured and sealed behind them, the angels will remotely fill the entire facility with Loki's Breath. This will ensure no outside interference. The angels will then in-struct Odin to take full control of the facility and feed all data back to mission control on a high-speed, secure channel.

"Thirteen: After your three months of undisturbed 'sleep,' the angels will return to wake you.

"Fourteen: After the angels have done a full medical evalu-ation on each of you to ensure that you have no adverse side-effects, you'll board the craft that you arrived on and return to the International Space Station.

"Fifteen: You'll spend a month more at the station, being evaluated—both medically and for the retention of the input you received while you slept.

"Sixteen: You'll board the reentry vehicle for your return to Earth.

"Seventeen: Once back on Earth, you'll be debriefed and get ready for your press conference. However, at no time are you to mention the Valhalla mission until you're given clearance—not even at your press conference after returning to Earth. We want to go over all the data collected and then hold a separate press conference, later on, with you present. At that second press conference, you'll each be able to talk about your experiences during the mission on the space station and about whatever has by that point been declassified about your time at the Valhalla station.

"Eighteen: You'll have the first press conference. It will occur at the Universal Space Center, and the president will be there with you.

"Nineteen: You'll go on a vacation—a world tour—completely at the government's expense. After the world tour, you'll be able to go home and do talk shows or whatever you wish until our second press conference about the mission. Any questions?" Geoff asked.

As the kids' hands all shot up, Robert stated, "I'm sure there are and will be questions that can be answered later. For now, I suggest we enjoy the rest of the flight and get something to eat before we arrive in Florida."

"Good idea," Geoff agreed. "Who wants to play video games, watch movies, or read?"

A chorus of "Me!" rang out from the kids as everyone rose from their seats and headed for the dining facility.

Chapter 3

Arrival and Tour in Florida

"APPROACHING UNIVERSAL Space Center" came over the overhead intercom.

"Thank you," Geoff responded to the cockpit. He then turned to the MacMurchaids and said, "Okay, everyone, let's all head to our seats and prepare for landing." After everyone was seated and buckled in, Geoff turned on a viewing console. "We'll be able to get a view of the area as we approach." Everyone watched as images of the entire complex appeared on the console. "We'll give you a tour of the center after everyone has rested. Then, we'll head to a hotel and to different theme parks for a real vacation. What do you think?" Geoff asked, suspecting he already knew the kids' answer.

A resounding chorus of "Yeah!" from the MacMurchaid children rang throughout the room.

Within minutes, the plane landed at the Universal Space Center, and everyone disembarked to find a waiting vehicle. "You'll be guests here on the base," Geoff informed everyone. "We'll first give you a tour of the space center and then move you to one of the hotels via bus. Remember that you cannot talk about the mission or Valhalla. You're on vacation, remember? We want you to enjoy yourselves as much as possible before your training starts. Do you think you can enjoy your vacation?"

Before anyone could respond, Robert held his hand up to keep everyone quiet. "I think I can answer for all of us, and the answer is yes. I'm sure we all understand what's at stake. We'll keep our mouths shut and be on our best behavior." He looked at his family, and they all nodded their agreement. "One thing, though. What are we going to wear? I mean, we can't go walking about wearing these uniforms all the time—unless, of course, there is a *Star Trek®* convention going on for the next few weeks. Plus, we only brought a few things of our own."

"Don't worry, Robert," Geoff reassured him. "Everything has been taken care of. Your clothes will arrive at the hotel while you're taking your tour. And tomorrow, you can wear the clothes you entered the Hercules in. They'll be clean and ready for you in the morning. As for tonight, we have provided some night clothes for you. Hopefully, you'll like them. As Tony said to Denise during our flight, 'Don't get your undies in a bundle.'"

The MacMurchaids arrived at the guest quarters to find someone waiting for them. It was Tom Hollett—Robert's best friend during their time at McConnell Air Force Base in Wichita, Kansas, when they served together as launch crew members for the Titan II Intercontinental Ballistic Missile. "Hello, Robert!" he called out. "How are you doing? Long time, no see."

"Well, hello, Tom! What the heck are *you* doing here?!"

"Waiting to see you, of course. Aren't you going to introduce me?"

"Sorry. Tom, you already know Denise. And this is Kris and Tony, who you might remember from when they were little tykes. And this is Troy and Nicole."

"Hello, I'm glad to see you again and meet you."

"Honey, you remember my best friend in the Air Force, Tom Hollett?"

"Well, yes, of course. I'm glad to see you again, Tom," Denise greeted him.

"Tony, this is your godfather. He helped keep me sane while I was waiting for you to be born. Of course, you do not remember him since you and Kris were both babies when I left the service. He was my enlisted counterpart on the Titan II four-man launch crew. We even talked about purchasing one of the old Titan II complexes when they became decommissioned, but you already know what happened to that idea." Robert's family had read the newspaper articles, seen photographs, and watched videos of all except one of the Titan II missile silos having their tops imploded, burying and sealing all entryways. Robert and a number of the Titan II veterans were glad that one of the Titan II sites, out near Tucson, Arizona, had been turned into a museum, though.

"Boy, they both have grown!" Tom remarked. "What do you feed them, Miracle Grow?"

"Well, the last time you saw them was thirteen years ago," Robert pointed out. "We were both just young men then."

"What are you saying, Robert, that we're old now? I don't

know about you, but I'm not over the hill yet."

"Oh, to heck with you, Tom. I'm just glad to see you. Where is your wife, Janice?"

"We'll see her later. She's eager to meet you and your family. As far as your earlier question, about what I'm doing here, I'm in the astronaut program. Once they decommissioned the old bird, I was able to specialize, take the officers' training corps, and work my way to captain."

"I'll be darned. Congratulations! We'll have to talk about old times over a game of spades and a few good imported cigars. Any good tobacco shops around here?"

"Before you travel down memory lane, let's get to the facts at hand," Geoff interrupted. "Tom has volunteered to help train you and your family for the mission. Since you two are already good friends and he's with the program, it works out perfectly. But right now, why don't we get everyone settled in and head to dinner?"

"Okay, Congressman Pitts," Tom agreed. He then turned to Robert. "Janice and I will meet you and your family in the dining area later. We'll talk more then."

"Okay, Tom. See you then." Robert and Tom shook hands and hugged each other. As Tom left, Robert turned to Geoff. "So, what's the hurry? The day is still young, and it isn't even close to dinner time."

"I want to show everyone to their rooms, and I need to see you privately."

"Privately? More secrets and catches?!" Denise sternly cut in.

"Honey—" Robert started to say before Geoff cut him off.

"Just a few minor details that pertain to Robert, specifically," Geoff informed Denise. "After those details are taken care of, I'll be glad to provide them to you as well, at dinner tonight."

"Okay, I guess," Denise reluctantly agreed. "But no more secrets from my family and me from here on. Is that understood?"

"Yes, ma'am." Geoff came to attention and saluted Denise. Everyone laughed.

After taking his family members to their rooms, Robert followed Geoff to the base commander's office. Seeing where they were, Robert realized the seriousness of the situation and tried to mentally prepare himself for what might come next. After introductions and pleasant greetings, Geoff began to explain things to Robert.

"You know that now, not all astronauts are military. In fact, an increasing number of them are from the civilian sector. Your family members are all civilians, but you're a veteran, which puts you in a special situation. So, the question is, do you go on a mission like this as just a civilian, or are you willing to retake your oath and become an active member of the United States Air Force again? Now, think about it before you answer. As civilians, you and your family will still have forms to sign and must follow certain directives. But if you choose to re-up, you'll then have to follow orders like any other airman. The choice is yours and yours alone. We would like to have a family with one active-duty member on this mission, but it isn't a prerequisite. We'll give you a little time to decide before we begin your family's training."

"I do not need any time to decide," Robert stated. "Denise and I have talked about me wanting to return to service over the years, but there was always one item or another that kept me from doing it. For example, I had too many dependents as far as military regulations were concerned. The only way they would have let me rejoin was to divorce Denise and sign the kids over to her. I could then rejoin and, after a period of time, remarry Denise. But I was unwilling to do that per the chance that something might happen to keep us from becoming a whole family again. I'm a family man, and a family man I'll be until the day I die, whether I'm able to rejoin or not. If I'm allowed to rejoin the Air Force without having to separate from my family, then I will happily retake my oath. But if I must separate from my family for any reason just to rejoin, then I will say no. That's my answer. So, I guess the ball is in the Air Force's and United States government's court as to what they want to do."

"I had a feeling that might have been your reason for not returning to service prior to this, but I wasn't sure," Geoff responded. "So, in anticipation of this possible response from you, I worked to get an executive waiver for any regulations that would have prevented your return. I had hoped it was just the regulations that were holding you back from returning and not that you had no interest in returning. So, if you're willing, I'll hand the executive order to the colonel, and he can administer the oath of enlistment. Or should I say he can administer the commissioning oath, as you'll be rejoining as an officer for this mission? This commission will become permanent on the completion of your family's mission and after the final press conference. Are you willing to take the oath here and now, Robert?"

"It would be my honor to take the oath in memory of my ancestors, both warriors and service members, throughout history—those who have served this country, are now serving, were wounded during service, and were taken during service," Robert confirmed. "I also do this for my family. As far as I am concerned, the oath I took all those years ago has not expired. But what I do now is a reaffirmation of that oath."

"Okay then. Colonel Devers, here is the executive order waiving any and all regulations which had previously prevented Robert's return to duty. Will you now administer the oath of commissioning?" Geoff asked him.

"Yes, I will, Congressman Pitts." The colonel turned to Robert. "Raise your right hand and repeat after me. I, state your name."

"I, Robert Edward MacMurchaid."

"Having been appointed an officer in the service of the United States."

"Having been appointed an officer in the service of the United States."

"As indicated above in the grade of captain, do solemnly swear."

"As indicated above in the grade of captain, do solemnly swear."

"That I will support and defend the Constitution of the United States against all enemies, both foreign and domestic."

"That I will support and defend the Constitution of the United States against all enemies, both foreign and domestic."

"That I will bear true faith and allegiance to the same."

"That I will bear true faith and allegiance to the same."

"That I take this obligation freely, without mental reservations or purpose of evasion."

"That I take this obligation freely, without mental reservations or purpose of evasion."

"And that I will well and faithfully discharge the duties of the office upon which I am about to enter."

"And that I will well and faithfully discharge the duties of the office upon which I am about to enter."

"So help me God."

"So help me God."

"You may lower your hand, Robert," the colonel instructed him.

"Thank you, sir." And with the oath finished, Robert saluted the colonel out of proper respect.

The colonel returned the salute and asked, "You realize that since you aren't in uniform yet, you don't have to salute me?"

"I know, sir. But I do it as a sign of respect and thanks."

"Don't thank me yet. You might end up hating the fact that you're back in the military!"

"I might hate the circumstances, sir. But being back in I won't hate."

Geoff interrupted the conversation, saying, "Robert, we need you to sign some papers that are normally completed before the oath. We did not have you sign them beforehand because we wanted to surprise you with your new rank, Captain MacMurchaid. After you finish signing, we'll go get you into dress blues with your new rank to attend tonight's dinner in. Won't Denise be surprised?"

"She probably will be, but she has always liked seeing me dressed up. But what will my instructor, Tom, think since he had to work his way up through the ranks?" Robert asked as he signed all the paperwork in the required places.

"He already knew what your rank would be if you accepted our offer. He didn't want to be your superior. He still considers you his equal and his friend. Finished signing? Good, let's go prepare the dinner surprise for your family."

"But it won't be much of a surprise if I go to dinner with them already in my dress blues."

"You won't go to dinner *with* them, Robert," Geoff informed him. "Instead, I have an airman who will escort your family to the dining area. He'll tell them we were delayed and that we'll join them there shortly." With that, Geoff and the colonel escorted Robert to get his dress uniform fitted.

An airman knocked on the door of Robert and Denise's room. Denise answered the door, saying, "Hello."

"Good evening, ma'am," the airman said. "I've been sent to escort you and your family to the dining area."

"Well, my husband isn't here yet. Maybe we should wait for him to get here first?"

"I've been told that he and Congressman Pitts were delayed and will meet you and your family in the dining area. If you would come with me and gather your children, ma'am? You have people waiting to see you in the dining area."

"Okay," Denise said hesitantly. "Let me just grab a few things and get my children." After picking up a few necessities and her bag, Denise and the airman got the children from their rooms and headed to the dining area. When they arrived at the dining area, Denise saw Tom and a woman who she was sure must be Janice. But there was also a surprise: Geoff had apparently arranged for Denise's folks—Robert's dad and stepmother and stepsister, Robert's mom and stepfather, and Robert's brother—to be there.

After hugs and greetings, the senior Robert MacMurchaid asked, "What in the Sam Hill is going on? We were all met by government officials and escorted to flights bound for here. But nobody is saying anything—not even a hint. And now, we find out that you all are here, too. And where is Robert?"

"I can answer your questions, Dad," Robert said as he walked through a door at the other end of the room. He was in full dress blues with his hat in his hand. "You're here for a couple of special announcements that cannot be given to the public yet but can be given to close family and certain friends." He nodded toward Tom. "One announcement, as you as can see, is that I am re-enlisted in the Air Force—not as a senior airman as I was at my honorable discharge but as a captain. The rest I will let Geoff explain." Everyone headed over to greet Robert. They were still a little shocked but were happy.

Geoff took over, saying, "I think we should all eat first, and then I'll bring the rest of you up to speed as to what is happening here."

Once everyone had eaten and visited with each other a little, Geoff started the same presentation he had given on the flight down but requested that everyone hold comments and questions until he was through. This time, the presentation was slightly modified to remove any mention of the Valhalla portion of the mission. Once Geoff finished the presentation, there were definitely questions and comments, some colorfully worded. Robert and Denise's relatives questioned their sanity for agreeing to, as Robert's brother worded it, "this madness."

Robert eventually had to interject to put an end to the maddening conversation and try to bring peace back to the room. "All right! Everyone! Please sit down?! I'm going to make this as clear as possible. You raised us to be responsible and careful, but even in everyday life, there are no guarantees that we'll not get hurt or killed. It could happen without leaving Earth's gravity. My family knows of the dangers of space travel because we have either seen or studied the deaths of American and other astronauts. I've also educated my children on the deaths in the Soviet Union's space program. I want them to keep up with all things happening on this little blue marble as well as into space, whether it involves the moon, Mars, an asteroid, or the entire universe. Each and every family member knows I will not put their lives in danger, and you all know Denise would kill me if I did."

Chuckles could be heard around the room after that last statement, especially with Denise nodding her head in agreement with it. Robert continued, saying, "Since a number of family members here are veterans and are still active with the military in some fashion, everyone in this room should know of the security reasons this mission cannot be discussed outside of certain locations. Now, let's enjoy the rest of the evening together. Geoff, are we *all* going to tour the Universal Space Center?"

"Yes, Robert. And we'll make a special stop at one location in particular. It's one of those locations where we remember certain family members of our astronaut program who were lost." Everyone in the room realized that the location Geoff was referring to was where Apollo 1 was doing ground tests when a fire broke out in the capsule filled with pure oxygen, killing the crew (Virgil "Gus" Grissom, Edward White, and Roger Chaffee). "I'm sure everyone will enjoy the tour tomorrow since we'll take you to some locations that most of the public doesn't visit. We'll start the tour shortly after breakfast. For now, please enjoy the rest of the evening."

After a little time for conversation, Geoff directed everyone's attention to the big screen at the end of the room. "I figured you might enjoy seeing some shows and clips from different periods of time during the history of the space program. We'll start with some movies with animated characters, featuring Werner von Braun, and then move into some features that were used to help gain support for the space program during its early days. Some of us old folks will remember some of these videos, but other videos were made before even we were born. So, we aren't as old as you kids might think we are!" More laughter echoed throughout the room. As the laughter subsided, the first feature began.

* * *

Once everyone was awake, up, and had eaten a good breakfast, they gathered together for the promised tour. Geoff explained, "Before we get started, I want to provide you with some background information about the tour you'll be going on. First, this tour will be conducted under special permission since some areas we'll visit are restricted. Second, some of the locations will not look like much since a number of launch facilities were deconstructed once they were no longer in use. Third, we cannot get behind schedule since we could end up in the way of crews that will be preparing a launch pad for a future launch.

"Since Robert and Tom are old Titan II missile men, we'll stop by Launch Pad 19, where the Titan II was launched as the lift vehicle for the Gemini spacecraft. There are other pads where Titan II vehicles were used for other purposes, and we'll drive by those ones. As I said yesterday, we'll stop at Launch Pad 34 to pay our respects. I know that stopping there will make some of you nervous about this mission, but it should help instill the importance of what this family is about to do. Okay, let's load everyone into the tour vehicles."

Everyone got into the vehicles, and the tour headed to the south end of the cape to begin. Geoff reminded everyone about the early days when Werner von Braun and his fellow scientists began testing rockets to launch men out of Earth's atmosphere. There were catastrophic and non-catastrophic failures during a number of tests. Some of the designs would become part of America's missile defense, some would help improve our communications capabilities, some would aid in learning more about our planet, and then there were those that would propel our first astronauts into space.

As Geoff had promised, they first stopped at Pad 19 for Tom and Robert to get a better realization that the missile they had worked on played roles other than just national defense.

On the way there, they passed other pads from which the Titan II had been launched for other purposes. After a few minutes, the tour continued to its next scheduled stop, at Pad 34, where America lost Grissom, White, and Chaffee during ground testing. During the stop, everyone paid their respects in their own way to those men as well as others who had died throughout mankind's reach into space. Once everyone was ready, the tour continued past other pads, various buildings, and finally back to the space center's main control center.

At the main control center, everyone headed inside while Geoff explained, "This is where we'll monitor you while you're in your spacecraft up to and during launch. At a certain time after lift-off, Houston will take over the operation of monitoring you and coordinating with our monitoring stations around the world. Just like fully-certified astronauts, you'll have bio-monitors on you to see if you're doing fine medically. That way, we can know at any point during your trip if you're go or no-go to continue in the mission.

"Besides this being historical having an entire family in space, your four children will be the first astronauts under our height standards and the first human children to fly into space. They'll be setting the future standards and paving the way for the possibility of future children getting to do what you're about to do. Scientists, politicians, teachers, parents, and the people of Earth will be looking up to you in more than one sense. So, be at your best—for the MacMurchaids, that is." Everyone laughed, even if the children looked somewhat puzzled at Geoff's joke.

"Now that the tour is basically over," Geoff continued,

"let's get you back to your quarters so you can get ready to start your actual vacation tomorrow and be rested for all that is ahead of you."

Chapter 4

The Promised Vacation

A FTER THE TOUR, everyone had their bags packed and ready so that they could stay at a hotel near the theme parks. Geoff asked Robert, "Did you make sure everyone left their clothes related to the mission in their quarters? And I mean *everyone*, including yourself. I know you like having an Air Force uniform again."

Robert mockingly replied, "Yes, Papa Geoff," looking as if he were a pouting child. Laughter and giggles could be heard from everyone else.

"All right now, enough of that," Geoff said, pretending as though he were scolding Robert. Now everyone was in full laughter mode.

With everyone and everything loaded into hotel vans, the group headed to the hotel. After arriving there, an Air Force official in street clothes handed Geoff the keys to the suites. "Okay, everyone, this way." Geoff led them to an elevator. When they got off the elevator and entered the main suite, everyone realized that their vacation had started. "As you were told, nothing other than the vacation may be mentioned to anyone," Geoff reminded everyone. "Tomorrow, you'll be taken to a theme park for a day of fun. After that, you'll go to the next theme park and spend a couple of days there since there is so much to do there.

"While here at the hotel," Geoff continued, "your meals and some snacks will be brought to this suite. Your rooms are adjoining from these doors. We want you to enjoy this vacation as if you planned it yourselves. And if you get bored or find that you can't sleep, there are plenty of movies to watch, video games to play, and books to read. Tomorrow, you'll have an early wake-up call so you can eat and get ready for a full day of fun."

"Uh, Geoff, are we allowed to go swimming while we're here at the hotel?" Kris asked. "Because you're making it sound as if we're not allowed to do anything unless we're at the parks or here in these rooms. It almost feels and sounds like we're prisoners, and you're the warden."

"No, you're not prisoners. And yes, you may go swimming. But also yes, you must still follow some rules. And finally, yes, I will be your acting warden, and there will be people watching you like guards—mainly for your safety. Your mom and dad will be the ones to make sure you don't slip up and spill the beans ahead of schedule," Geoff informed Kris with a grin.

Denise, adding to what Geoff said, pointed out, "What Geoff and the others might do if you slip up won't be anything in comparison to what Daddy and I might do." She turned and gave Geoff a wink.

36

The MacMurchaids dispersed to their rooms to unpack, rest, and get ready for their first big day of vacation. "I wonder how our folks are managing this," Denise pondered out loud. "I mean, they're on their way back to their homes, and we're here. It's a lot to take in, and we've had more time than them to let it sink in. It still hasn't fully sunken in with me, so I know it hasn't with them."

"I don't know, honey," Robert responded. "They'll each see it in their own way. I know they'll have questions and worries about what we'll be doing. But let's not worry about that now. Let's try to just enjoy ourselves. After all, we're on vacation, remember?" Robert tried his best to put Denise more at ease. But even he hadn't fully processed the details in his mind. Since he usually planned ahead for things, he knew they would encounter problems and questions that would have to be addressed. But for now, he would have to let the next few days flow as they may. For now, he was a dad and a husband on vacation with his family, doing what most dads do: handling spats and enforcing parental law. "All right, everyone, we'll be ready for bed by 10 and in bed no later than midnight. That means asleep. Because if I know our host, that wake-up call will be around 5:30 to 6 a.m."

* * *

"Up and at 'em, kids! Mom and I got the wake-up call," Robert announced to his children. "Just like I figured, it came at 5:30 a.m. Let's move it so we can eat because they want to let us into the park before it officially opens. They want to make sure we have time to plan what attractions we want to visit and get as many of them in as possible. They're pulling strings that are not available to the general public. Let's do our part to make this day one of the best days of our lives."

The kids slowly began to motivate, get dressed, and use the bathroom. At 6 a.m., a knock came at the suite's main door. It was room service pushing in two carts loaded with breakfast items. "You kids better hurry up and eat," Robert suggested. "Otherwise, Mom and I will become fat and sassy old people."

Tony responded from one of the bathrooms, saying, "But Dad, you're already sassy and way older than us." Giggles could be heard coming from his siblings. Robert ignored the comment . . . this time.

All four MacMurchaid children emerged from their room at the same time. Their eyes were wide at the sight of the breakfast choices on the carts. The carts were piled high with an assortment of doughnuts, small cereal boxes, bacon, toast, packets of jellies and jams, milk, juice, cocoa mix, coffee, and a few extra items. "I want mocha!" Troy shouted. Everyone dug in and ate more than they should because this was breakfast heaven.

An hour after the breakfast arrived, another knock came at the suite's main door. This time it was Geoff. "Hello everyone," he greeted them.

Robert greeted Geoff back and said, "I would offer you some breakfast and coffee, but as you can see, there isn't much left on either cart."

"I figured there might be some coffee left when I arrived, Robert. But you're telling me that you and Denise drink that much in the morning?!"

"No, the kids wanted mocha, and that was where the majority of the coffee went. I just hope that much caffeine doesn't cause them to sleep through our time at the park. During a normal school week, they don't get coffee and seldom any cocoa. The teachers already complain that they're falling asleep by second hour anyway."

"Well," Geoff responded, "I don't think they'll fall asleep today since the park is much more exciting than school."

"Yes!" Troy yelled, voicing his agreement.

"We've hired a photographer to take photos of you all enjoying your vacation," Geoff informed everyone. "As far as this person is concerned, though, you won this vacation and the photos may be used for a magazine spread or at the least newspapers back in Oklahoma. What she *doesn't* know is the actual details behind why we want the photos, and we want to keep it that way. Okay?" All of the MacMurchaids indicated their agreement. "Good. Let's head down to your transportation for today's fun."

Everyone headed down to the lobby and out the door to a waiting vehicle. After a short ride to the park, they noticed two gentlemen standing just inside the gate. The men were dressed like Jake and Elwood, The Blues Brothers. The kids were saying, "Cool," "All right," and "Neat."

Once the vehicle stopped, everyone began to pile out and gather together. "These gentlemen have agreed to escort you for a while this morning," Geoff said, referring to The Blues Brothers. "But they can't be with you all day because they have some gigs to play. Once they leave you, you're on your own to enjoy yourselves. Have a great day while you're here, and I'll meet you later, at the hotel. I'm not on vacation like you are. Some of us still have to work for a living!"

"I know you're a politician, but you don't have to lie to us, Geoff," Robert said jokingly as Geoff turned to go. Geoff just smiled and waved to them.

"Now, the fun begins!" Nicole shouted.

Denise and Robert looked at each other, wondering, as many parents do, how much fun it would actually be for them. Robert finally said, "At least there will be others in the crowd helping us keep eyes on these four."

"I don't know if the others are ready for our four or not," Denise replied with a worried grin on her face. "Hopefully, all that mocha they drank this morning will work like usual for them and slow the four tornadoes down a bit. Otherwise, the team assigned to us might have to call in a couple of other teams or at least a specialty unit."

"Let's hope for the best, and I'm sure our kids will do fine," Robert reassured her. "We can hope that this first day will start them on an easy down wave for the rest of this vacation." Robert gave Denise a supportive hug and kiss.

Just then, they heard the familiar sound of a camera going off. "Hello, I'm Tamara. I've been assigned to document the vacation you won photographically."

Everyone said hello to Tamara. Denise then said to Tamara, "I hope those are your running shoes you have on because once these four get going, they're hard to keep up with." Denise smiled at her own joke.

Tamara responded nervously, "Uh, yes, they are. Could we get a group photo with everyone together?" She waved to the gentlemen in Blues Brothers clothing, indicating that they should join the photo. Once the picture had been taken, each family member and Tamara had a special wristband put on their wrists.

Robert said, "Now . . . let the excitement begin!" And they all headed through the front gate and into the park. There were rides to ride, there were attractions to be seen, and there was food to be eaten.

Tamara soon began to see what Denise and Robert had warned her about and wondered if she was up to the task of following the children for an entire week. She asked Robert if this was normal for their family on vacations.

Robert responded, "We've never been on a vacation like this before. Our vacations have been going to one of the lakes in Oklahoma, camping somewhere near streams or woods, going to powwows, or maybe going to zoos or fairs. Most of our outings have been in Oklahoma and Arkansas. So, in answer to your question, I have no real answer. All I know is we're supposed to visit nearly all of the theme parks within the one week we're down here for this vacation. I'm hoping the kids will gradually begin to slow down a little each day from the previous day's activities, but sometimes, the children seem to recharge before each event."

"So, this is a first for all of you?" Tamara asked.

"Yes. This is the beginning of something really big for all of us," Robert responded.

"Honey, maybe you shouldn't get ahead of yourself about this," Denise warned him, giving him a wink and a nod. "You might scare her."

Robert understood what his wife was really alluding to and gave her a nod of understanding. "Denise and I will enjoy some of the attractions and maybe take in a ride or two each day, but this will be mostly an adventure for our children. I just hope the parks can contain that much enthusiasm." Robert chuckled.

Though they were let into the park early, it didn't seem like they were there long before the rest of the tourists had filled the park. "As we tried to warn you, with the enthusiasm our bunch has, time does fly," Denise explained to Tamara. "I hope you have the endurance for the rest of today, much less the rest of this week. With the crowds here, it will be hard at times to keep track of our children. But luckily, they do try to keep us informed where they'll be and in what order they plan on doing things."

"Aren't you worried something might happen to one or more of them?" Tamara asked.

"We constantly worry about them whether we're back home or anywhere," Robert explained. "The main worry is for someone to try something, but with this bunch, that person might be taken to a hospital before going to jail. We made sure they each know how to take care of themselves and each other. They can take care of themselves in a clean fashion or fight dirty with whatever is available."

After what seemed like a long day for the photographic reporter, the family gathered to head back to the hotel. Though the excitement was still high, everyone was ready for a good night's rest before the next day. And after a week of traveling to more parks, everyone seemed to have settled down compared to when they first arrived at the hotel. Tamara told Robert and

Denise, "I'll be heading back home now to share the photos and story of your vacation through the newspapers and other media. I hope to see you again sometime, back in Oklahoma."

"Oh, we're sure we'll meet again," Robert replied. "But we won't be heading back right away as a friend down here wants us to stay a little longer. I'm sure the person who asked you to cover our vacation this week will be back in contact with you. Meantime, we hope you enjoy your flight back."

Everyone said goodbye to Tamara. Once she was gone, Robert gathered the family together. "I guess we better get some rest tonight before our friend comes to pick us up for our next adventure!" he said.

Chapter 5

Trip to Washington, DC

THE NEXT MORNING, the MacMurchaid family was awakened around 5:30 a.m. to get ready and have breakfast. While everyone was finishing up what they were doing, a knock came at the door. When the door opened, a couple of men in suits and ties were standing there.

"Congressman Pitts and Captain Hollett are unable to be here this morning as they were called to DC last night," the men informed Robert. "We were sent to escort you and your family to a private jet that is waiting to take you to meet them. Don't worry about your things here. A team is ready to take everything back to the space center. If you'll follow us, we're on a time schedule and hope to keep to it. For your safety and for security reasons, we'll exit the hotel via a different route than you're used to."

Everyone nodded their agreement with the instructions. The men in suits took the entire family to a waiting van, which looked like one belonging to the hotel. Once everyone was in and secure, the van left the premises via a back way. Not long after, they were at a private airfield and boarded the jet that had been standing by for them.

Once the jet was airborne, a video screen at the front of the cabin came on. It was a video message from Geoff. "Sorry I'm not there to give you this message personally," he said, "but Tom and I had to get to Washington ahead of you to get preparations completed for your arrival. Once you land, you'll be taken to a hotel and checked into your suites. Within an hour or two, I'll stop by to escort you on a tour of our nation's capital, including a few sites I know you'll find particularly interesting. Tomorrow is your day to shop and do what you want, but you'll need to be back to your suites by 4 p.m. because I'll be there around 5 to pick you up for a dinner engagement. This dinner isn't formal, but it isn't casual either. We've taken the opportunity to order each of you a leisure suit or dress for the occasion. I'll see you shortly. Until then, please enjoy your flight." Then, the screen went blank.

"Well, wasn't that short and sweet," Denise said with some sass, slightly put off by the message. "I guess we'll enjoy another tour. But why are they being hush-hush with us so much considering our lives are on the line for this 'adventure?'"

"Honey, with technological advancements and lower levels of trust in the world, nowadays they cannot take too many chances revealing too much," Robert pointed out. "I have my suspicions as to what events they're preparing for, and if I'm correct in those suspicions, then they just want to keep us as safe as they can." Robert knew that if word of the family's mission got out to the world, there were individuals and governments that might try to sabotage it and would relish in the

United States having a major failure. He suspected Denise already knew what was really going on anyway.

Landing outside the capital, the jet taxied to a hangar where the family was escorted to a vehicle that was ready to take them to their hotel. The drive from the hangar to the hotel almost seemed longer than the flight did. They were escorted from the garage to their suites, where they had snacks while waiting for Geoff to arrive.

True to his word, Geoff showed up a little over an hour after the MacMurchaids had arrived at the hotel. "Ready for a tour of the town and surrounding area?" he asked.

"Yeah!" The children shouted in near unison. Denise and Robert nodded their heads in agreement as well.

"Well, we have a route figured out that will allow us to see as much as possible today. And what we don't see today, we'll see later. Okay?" Geoff looked at everyone to make sure they seemed ready to depart. "Let's head down to our ride and begin the tour."

After everyone had loaded into a van, Geoff continued, "A few of the attractions we'll have to just drive by without stopping since there's so many here to see and we have a tight schedule to keep. But don't worry, we'll stop at plenty of sites and monuments where you can get out and walk around. And we'll even take a ride to Arlington National Cemetery, just outside the city. I hope everyone is wearing comfortable walking shoes!" Geoff had taken a peek at everyone's feet before they left, so he already knew they were in good shape in that regard.

"Our first stop will be at the National Air and Space Museum since it relates to everything we've talked about over the last week," Geoff continued. "Then, we'll take a walk and see some of the monuments and memorials that are near the museum. Don't worry; we'll take it easy on the walk and take breaks here and there. Then, we'll get back into our ride and head to Arlington National Cemetery. If there's still a little time left at the end of the day, we might even take a trip over to the National Zoological Park."

The children were already discussing amongst themselves how excited they were for the day's trip. As for Denise, she was just worried about all the walking since she had seen maps of the area and knew they would be getting a workout from it. Robert, realizing that Denise was quiet and appeared deep in thought, leaned closer to her and softly said, "I know that today will be a lot of stairs and walking, honey. But Geoff did guarantee that we would take breaks. It might wear you and me out but look at this way: it might also wear the kids down to the point that they might go to bed early for once." Denise grinned at that idea.

"We've arrived," Geoff announced.

Robert responded, "Now, let the leg workout begin!" Denise huffed and cut her eyes at him.

After they entered the museum, Geoff said, "As we go through here, there will be some items that are originals and others that are duplicates. I've been here a number of times, but I still get the feeling I've traveled in a time machine when I see these items from the past. Though we'll see some things related to your next adventure, they'll be nowhere near as advanced as the items you'll soon become familiar with." Turning to the children, he said, "Some of the things you'll see here will be what your parents and I saw on television as we were growing up."

Kris responded, "Oh, there was television at Kitty Hawk?" He laughed at his own joke.

"Ha, ha. So funny, I forgot to laugh," Denise responded dryly. "Maybe we'll let you out through an airlock like a bad guy in one of your dad's favorite sci-fi movies," Denise quipped, giving a raised eyebrow toward Kris.

"No, honey, don't say that," Robert jumped in. "The kids will think they'll be stars after our mission. But we could make them *shooting* stars on the way back if they get out of control." Robert gave all the kids an evil grin and evil laugh.

The children knew their dad was kidding, but the youngest ones nevertheless thought, *What if he means it?*

"Now, now, there will be none of that," Geoff responded. "You kids go ahead and look around. But don't touch anything unless it's permitted. Your mom, dad, and I will be walking around and talking."

As soon as Geoff finished his statement, he received a text message on his cell phone. After responding and getting a return response, he turned to Denise and Robert and said, "Let's take our time enjoying the sites here. Our timetable has shifted slightly. Nothing major, but we might have to shorten the overall tour today. I received a message that the president wants to have dinner tonight instead of tomorrow night. Word is he wants to meet you and your family and get your perspective on the upcoming mission. He sometimes likes to do things like this if he's writing his own speech for a press conference. I want the two of you to be prepared for questions he might ask. Do you think you're up to the task?"

Robert and Denise were grinning with excitement. Even though they had suspected they might meet the president, they were thrilled to hear it confirmed. "I can't speak for Denise," Robert said, "but I've been preparing myself for this possibility since we were told about the dinner and press conference. I have a sometimes-unfortunate trait of looking at an upcoming event and thinking of every possible thing that could happen or go wrong. That way, I can be as prepared as possible," Robert informed Geoff.

"I realize there will be a lot of questions asked at the press conference," Robert continued. "And I'll most likely need to speak beyond those questions. I somewhat understand what our astronauts and others in the public eye tend to go through being in the public eye. I also know that with the advancement in all forms of media, there will be those looking for juicy tidbits to exploit. I try not to worry my family with details about all the possibilities I consider. But now that I mention it here, perhaps I've added to Denise's stress level. What are you thinking, honey?"

"Well, I try not to overthink things as much as you do because I've always trusted you to be able to handle nearly everything we do. Yes, you just added to my stress level a bit. But it's nothing I can't handle. I'm just hoping that the only questions I receive from the president and at the press conference will require simple answers. Otherwise, I'm expecting you to step in and help me. Right now, I want to enjoy this gift of what we're doing and let the future happen in its own time.

Have you been keeping tabs on our children?"

"Yes, honey. They're a little spread out but well within my view," Robert assured her.

"Don't worry; we have a detail of both men and women in civilian clothing with us today," Geoff further assured her. "They're keeping everyone guarded and safe."

"But who's going to keep everyone and everything safe from our squad of hellions?" Denise said, sheepishly grinning as she attempted to lighten the mood.

"Well, we better catch up to those hellions and move this along," Robert suggested. "We should let them know about the change in plans so that they can enjoy their time here a little longer. Who knows how much longer they'll have to enjoy things like this without the press following them around."

"The press following them around?!" Denise exclaimed. "Oh, we'll definitely have to set them down and have a discussion as to how they'll be expected to act with that mess."

After gathering everyone together, Robert explained the changes to the schedule and that a further discussion would be held once they were back at the hotel.

Tony said, "Aww, okay. But can we still get a visit to the zoo in today? We want to at least enjoy it without all the cameras and questions."

Geoff assured them they would keep that on the schedule for the day. But he said that, in order to do so, they would have to shorten their walking tour a bit. Denise was somewhat happy to hear that.

"Understood!" Troy said on behalf of the children with a halfhearted salute as if he were an officer in the military.

"Okay, enough of that," Robert scolded him. He then turned to Geoff and mentioned, "After our family has its discussion at the hotel as to what to expect and what is expected from everyone, we'll get you a list of what monuments we want to go to."

Geoff responded, "That will work since I'm sure by then the press will be tagging along, and it will give us a day or two to make sure everyone is in position for your safety and security that day."

The group then headed outside to do a quick partial walkthrough of some of the nearby monuments before they loaded back into the van and headed to the National Zoological Park. The love of nature and its inhabitants was strong in the entire MacMurchaid family, so the children were extremely enthusiastic.

"Now, everyone remember that we don't have the full time we would like to have to see everything here in the park," Geoff reminded them. "We've been invited to dinner, and we don't want to make our host wait." With that, everyone headed into the park to see what they could see in the couple of hours they had before heading back to the hotel to dress for dinner.

Chapter 6

Dinner with the President

"DAD, WHY DO THEY call clothes like these leisure suits?" Troy asked, being his usual inquisitive self. "There's nothing relaxing about them except that you don't have to wear a tie. These are closer to what we would wear to church."

"Well, Troy, you pretty much answered your own question," Robert responded. "These types of suits allow you to be dressed up and respectful but without being all stuffy and business-like. Remember that we're meeting with the president of the United States and his wife. This is one way to show some respect to them and their position in relation to our government. Personally, I would rather be in my dress blues to meet them, but I respect their wishes and the fact that no one except for a select few people know what we're about to become—world celebrities. The day they make that announcement, you'll wish you were still wearing this instead of what you'll be wearing on that day."

Nicole, speaking to her mother, said, "I don't mind dresses

that much. But for dinner, I would rather wear something different—something more comfortable for me."

Denise glanced at her daughter and replied, "You'll find out as you get older that there are certain events that call for you to wear dresses. And as you get older, you'll find yourself wanting to wear dresses to impress some people, to be respectable, and to one day attract or make an impression on a possible boyfriend."

"Ewww, Mooom! You know how I feel about boys. I don't want to think that far ahead in life, and right now, you're being gross." Nicole was scowling.

"Sorry if you're grossed about it now, but these are the facts of life, Nicole. Some things you don't have to think about at your age, but somewhere and sometime during your life, these thoughts and things will happen. I'm just glad you've been taught with your brothers to handle bad situations." Denise finished her statement at the same time she finished getting herself and Nicole ready.

A knock came at the door of the main suite. Robert answered the door and saw that it was Tom Hollett. "I was expecting Geoff or one of the members of our detail, but I'm glad to see *you!*"

"Geoff got called back to Florida to start preparations down there," Tom explained. "But he'll be back for the press conference. So, I guess you and your family will have to enjoy the company of Janice and me for this evening's dinner engagement. Is everyone ready?"

"As ready as they'll ever be, I guess," Robert responded. "I'm guessing they would all rather be wearing more comfortable clothes, though. Denise and I would feel a little better wearing something more formal for this."

"Speak for yourself," Denise exclaimed. "This is quite fine for the occasion, as far as I'm concerned."

"Well, I'm just glad to see that I'm not the only military man who is not in uniform. Though, I do see you're dressed more formal than us, Tom," Robert noted.

"All right, Robert, let's get everyone downstairs and loaded in so we won't be late. My wife will be waiting for us there, and I don't want to upset her. I'd be more afraid of making her mad than making the president mad." Tom winked at Robert.

"I completely understand what you're saying," Robert responded. "It's all right for them to keep *us* waiting, but if we keep *them* waiting, hooo boy!" Tom and Robert laughed while Denise glared.

"I'll make sure I mention those comments to your wife, Tom," Denise teased, still glaring.

"*See*, Tom! You don't want to make them mad even if you're joking around." Robert and Tom laughed some more while the children all covered their mouths to hide their smiles from their mother.

Tom and the MacMurchaids headed downstairs and loaded into the vehicle that was waiting for them. They then proceeded to their dinner engagement. Pulling up to the venue, they realized they were not at a usual location designated for dinners with the president but instead at a gate to Fort McNair—an army facility. The guards there inspected the vehicle and checked the driver's credentials before waving the vehicle through.

Robert now realized that they were going to see more than just the president. And he now felt completely underdressed for the occasion. "Tom, how many of the top brass will be here this evening, and are all the branches represented tonight?"

Tom could see Robert was getting a bit nervous. "I don't know how many will be here or if all the branches of service will be represented. But relax; they were told that, for security reasons, you won't be in uniform tonight or until the press conference."

"That doesn't make me feel more at ease, Tom. I'll still be tempted to salute them even though I'm not in uniform." Robert hadn't been this nervous for as long as he could remember. "I think I might feel more comfortable if I was facing the MPs back at McConnell Air Force Base when the sector commander made a mistake on the crew's paperwork, and I was the one who delivered that paperwork!"

"That was a cold day in Kansas, wasn't it?" Tom said, grinning while trying to calm Robert down.

Denise interrupted, saying, "Why weren't Robert and I informed of the extra guests?"

Tom replied, "For the same security reasons that you're not being told much at all."

"Look, Tom, both Robert and I are military brats. He was a veteran until recently. We both understand the security risks and protocols involved. We would not mention this to our children or anyone else. But *we* have the need to know," Denise implored.

"I know both of you understand security protocol, Denise. But this decision came from the joint chiefs. If you want to be

55

mad at someone, you can take it up with them, though I don't think it would do any good. Besides, they have to make sure everyone's safety is covered with all the international tensions presently building." Tom wasn't very reassuring to Robert and Denise, and the children were now starting to get more of a sense of the importance and sensitivity of their upcoming so-called "adventure."

"Tom, you aren't very diplomatic, are you?" Robert chided him. "If the children had been more distracted, maybe they wouldn't have heard so much and be so incredibly nervous now." Robert turned to his children. "You all will be fine. So, calm down. You're all smart and have the abilities to figure out possibilities for different situations. That's why Mom and I gave you every chance to learn different things while growing up. Neither your mom nor I ever expected that we'd all be in a situation like this one, but we saw that it was out there as a possibility. Since we left home, we've been under constant observation and protection. A number of the people you met on our so-called vacation were there for your benefit, to protect all of us. Now, you can see how important you are—not only to Mom and me but to the future. But don't let this newfound importance go to your heads."

With that last sentence, the children started laughing. Nicole said, "All right, Daddy, we won't get the big head." Now everyone was laughing, including the driver, who up to this point had been very straitlaced and serious.

"Here we are," the driver announced. Everyone exited the vehicle and straightened their clothing.

Tom's wife, Janice, was waiting at the door. "Everyone inside is waiting, but I couldn't handle being in there any longer, so I came outside to wait for you," she said. "Hello, everyone." Everyone greeted Janice and immediately began treating her as though she were a part of the family, which made her feel good.

Everyone entered what, by all appearances, was the officers' mess and club. Once inside, they noticed that the tables were arranged so that the president, the first lady, and the top brass and their spouses would be seated at the main table. Other brass would be seated at the line of tables to the right. The line of tables to the left was apparently for the MacMurchaids and the Holletts, with room for maybe a few others.

After a short wait, the president finally arrived to greet the MacMurchaids, escorted by his security team. "I'm glad to finally meet you all in person," he said. "If you would, Captain MacMurchaid, would you please introduce me to your family?" As Robert did so, the president shook each family member's hand, greeted them, and welcomed them to the dinner.

"Sir, I fully understand the reason for security, but I feel a little underdressed for being in the company of all these superior officers," Robert stated.

"I understand, my boy," the president responded. "You're well within your rights to feel that way. But I'm glad you did as you were asked and did not wear your uniform."

"How could I refuse a request from the commander and chief, sir?" Robert answered back. "I'll do my best to act like a civilian and not salute each of these officers, though that will be hard to do since my military upbringing and training tells me to salute them out of respect."

"I understand your feelings on that since I was told that your lineage has a long line of servicemen in it," the president assured him. "Between you and me, I don't know if the officers will understand why you won't be saluting them. But I'll inform them before you meet them face to face that you're obeying orders and security protocol in that regard. Will that make it any easier for you?" the president asked Robert.

"It will help, sir, though the serviceman inside of me will still be fighting to get out," Robert answered.

The president let out a short laugh. "I like your response, Robert. It shows me you're an honorable and honest man." The president patted Robert on the shoulder.

After all the introductions were over and everyone was seated, the president said, "Let's eat before we have the question-and-answer session that everyone is expecting. I do have my own questions for your family, but they can wait. I assure you that they'll be simple and easy questions from me."

Then, plates of food were brought to all, and drinks were poured. The children were happy to see that their food was not what they were expecting. Apparently, word was passed on as to what each of them liked, including their favorite desserts and drinks. As for the adults, they were given small salads, fillet mignon, baked potatoes with the fixings, tea or coffee to drink, and pie ala mode for dessert. Conversation was abundant as everyone ate. As Robert and Denise observed the conversations, it seemed to them that everyone was having a pleasant time. Denise leaned over to Robert and whispered, "I sure hope everyone is still as pleasant during the question-and-answer session."

"For you and the children, I'm sure it will remain pleasant," Robert guessed. "And I suspect that once the officers finish questioning the five of you, they'll put all of you and Janice somewhere where you can relax. As for me, I'm prepared for the best, but I'm also ready for the worse. Maybe it will be somewhere in-between," Robert gently grabbed Denise's hand and held it. "For now, let's enjoy what's in front of us. We can be nervous later." He then kissed Denise on her cheek.

After everyone had eaten and the tables were cleared, the president said, "We'll give everyone a little time to let their food settle before we proceed." Most everyone got up and began walking around. A few people stepped outside for a smoke. Then, after about thirty minutes, everyone was called back in to be seated so that the question-and-answer session between the officers and the MacMurchaids could begin.

"We want to hear what each of you think about this project and what your feelings are about it," Tom informed the Mac-Murchaids. "We'll start with the children and Denise so that they can finish quickly and the children can enjoy the game room we set up specially for them while the wives visit with each other. Then, the officers and I will speak with Robert by himself."

Each child was asked simple questions, but everyone in the room was surprised to find that the children's answers were *not* so simple. In their answers, each child demonstrated extreme intelligence for their age. The officers then questioned Denise, and though the questions for her were not as simple, she answered them all straightforward. Denise's answers only gave the officers an inkling as to how her mind works, but they came to understand that she could be strong-willed and very protective. When the questions for Denise and the children had concluded, Janice and some other wives escorted Denise and the children from the room.

Then, it was Robert's turn to answer questions. One of the officers spoke up and said, "Knowing your previous military experience and security clearance, we know we can put our faith in you to do as you're told and keep your mission a secret."

"Yes, sir. You can," Robert confirmed.

Another officer followed with, "From what we heard and saw from your family, we can tell that you and your wife have been doing a fine job raising your children."

"Thank you, sir," Robert replied.

A third officer said, "Let us hear what your thoughts are on this mission."

Robert responded, "First of all, this mission is another important step in space exploration for all humankind. For me and some of my generation, we would say it's a long-overdue step to send an entire family into space. But I understand that the technology needed was not there during my youth, and we're much closer to having what we need now. And I don't use the word 'exploration' loosely either, sirs. Exploration has been there throughout history, though not all exploration has been fully noticed. For example, the names used for this mission come from Viking myths and legends. Many considered the Vikings to be raiders, but they were also explorers. They came to what would later be called the new world by many Europeans, long before Christopher Columbus was credited with finding it. There is proof of this in Oklahoma and other states."

"Before you continue with your answer, you said you feel what is happening now, with this mission, is long overdue. Please explain," another officer prodded Robert.

"I'd be glad to, sir. I grew up during the era of the US and USSR space race. We were just getting good with our observations on the moon as well as looking around the lunar surface for educational specimens when suddenly, our space programs stopped. I understand that people at that time were starting to think that going to the moon was becoming routine. But those of us who truly followed it and were interested understood otherwise. Many people, both civilians and those in politics, didn't like the cost of the space program. But people like me were willing to look past costs, to the future and to what possibilities lay ahead for space exploration. And sending an entire family to space is that future."

"I've already been informed and formed the opinion myself that you're an honest and honorable man, Robert," the president stated. "But these men, who are just getting to know you, haven't seen it yet. So, they might wonder if you're putting on airs to placate them."

"Sir, I come from a long line of servicemen and veterans. It would dishonor them if I put on airs. And I was raised by not just my parents but also my grandparents. They all taught me to be honest and to learn history. I still honor all of them by continuing to do so. As it has been said, those who do not learn from history are doomed to repeat it. I've learned more history outside of school than in it, thanks to those who raised me. So, if anyone thinks I'm putting on airs, then I suggest that another family be chosen to replace my family. As for keeping this project a secret, each oath I took—during my first enlistment and this new enlistment—has no expiration date. I will not dishonor my family and my ancestors, sirs." Robert finished and sat rigidly at attention in his seat.

"I don't think we need to replace your family, Robert," the president assured him. "I see your conviction about honor and those you choose to honor. You can relax and sit at ease. We'll cover some more questions and then let you join your family."

"Yes. Thank you, sir," Robert said respectfully.

For another thirty minutes or so, they continued the question-and-answer session. The officers found Robert's answers interesting, to say the least. But Robert could not tell from the officers' expressions whether they were fully satisfied with his answers. Finally, one of the officers announced that the session was over, that Robert could join his family in the game room, and that they would bring everyone back in a while.

"Yes, sirs. Thank you, sirs," Robert said as he rose from his chair to leave the room. He then joined his family and Janice in the game room. He watched the children play their games, and he stepped over to a pool table where he and Denise shot some pool until they were all called back to the dining hall.

Once everyone was seated again, the president stood and said, "We're all in agreement that this mission is a go with your family being the first full family sent into space. Since the press conference is still on the schedule for the day after tomorrow, you'll have tomorrow to relax and maybe finish the tour you started earlier. It's up to you. So, rest up for your big day being presented to the world! We'll see you again just before the press conference. Your driver will take you back to your hotel now. It was wonderful to meet you, and I hope you have a good night."

"Thank you, sir," Robert said on behalf of the MacMurchaid family. Denise and the children then individually thanked the president as well. They then headed out to their ride and returned to their hotel.

Once everyone was back in their suites and had gotten relaxed, Denise said to Robert, "That went better than I thought it would. The kids did exceptionally well answering their questions. I thought they would ask me harder questions. How did it go for you?"

"It went pretty much as I expected, though there was a rough spot or two during the start of it. I basically told them at one point that if they didn't think we're being honest with them about our enthusiasm for the mission, then they should find another family for it." Denise started to react to what Robert said, but then he said, "But they realized that we, especially me, weren't putting on airs. Apparently, someone had also informed them that you and I can be headstrong at times, but I think a few of the officers actually like that about us. I know the president liked it because it proves that we're the right choice as the family for this mission."

"Well, I, for one, am glad that is over, but I know we still have a lot ahead of us," Denise said as she sighed. She smiled at Robert, and they gave each other a goodnight kiss.

63

Chapter 7

The Press Conference

CONSIDERING HOW MUCH the MacMurchaid family had done since they left their home, the day after their dinner with the president, they decided not to go out and about but instead to stay at the hotel. Robert and Denise let the children play video games and watch television. And if anyone wanted to let off a little steam, they could head down to the indoor pool. They could eat their meals in the room or go down to the hotel restaurant. They were going to relax and enjoy the day as if they were back home. None of them wanted to think about the press conference the next day, but the thought of it remained in the back of their minds. The family's day otherwise went by calmly and pleasantly.

The day of the press conference finally arrived, and the family tried to treat the morning like it was any other routine morning. But still, they could not get the impending press conference out of their minds. After all, none of the family members had yet been grilled the way Robert had been during his question-and-answer session with the president and officers. Robert was mostly calm. He was only worried about his family first, upsetting his superior officers second, and lastly, bringing shame to any of his ancestors. He had written a few notes to carry with him during the press conference, but mostly, he planned to just speak from his heart. Once the family was dressed and ready, he gathered them for a prayer.

When the family finished its prayer, a knock came at the door. "Is that perfect timing or what?" Denise asked.

The gentleman who stood on the other side of the door stated, "Congressman Pitts sent me to drive you to the conference." Robert immediately noticed that this man was not one of the usual people who had been on duty watching over his family or acting as a driver. He stood in the doorway in front of the man, blocking the man's view of the rest of the family. He then signaled behind his back for Denise to move the family through a doorway to another suite. Hearing the ding of an elevator door, Robert peeked down the hallway to see the elevator door open. Geoff stepped out.

Robert immediately said, "Oh, hi, Geoff." The man at the doorway startled and turned to look toward the elevator, giving Robert a chance to put the man into a wrestling hold. Geoff ran over to see what was going on. Robert asked, "Geoff did you send this man for us?" The man tried to reach for something with his free hand, but Geoff stopped him.

"No!" Geoff responded. "I've never seen this man in my life."

Robert responded by increasing the pressure from his hold, causing the man to pass out. "Don't worry," Robert reassured Geoff, "he should revive soon so we can figure out who he is."

While the man was still passed out, Robert and Geoff searched him and found a gun, a knife, and some sort of device with a trigger. They also found a keycard for a different hotel, and Geoff immediately dispatched a team there to sweep it for devices. "He didn't look like any member of the details that have been watching us," Robert explained. "So, I kept him occupied at the door while Denise and the children moved to the next room."

The door of the elevator next to the one Geoff got off opened, and several security team members that Robert *did* recognize came rushing over. "Finish searching him," Geoff instructed them. "Here are the items we've recovered so far. He tried to get to this triggering device, so there might be explosives or chemical weapons nearby. Have a team check all security camera footage. Also look for accomplices he might have." Geoff then turned to Robert and said, "I see that age hasn't dulled your senses or your ability to act!"

"Well, when you have four children, your senses and reaction times are heightened over time," Robert said, half joking and half serious. "Let's go let Denise and the kids know that all is clear," he suggested. They headed into the suite and through the door that Denise and the children had gone through. "Okay, everyone. All is clear. I love you."

Denise responded, "I love you more. What was that all about?"

"Oh, just a minor bit of trouble," Geoff said, downplaying the seriousness of what had occurred.

"Don't worry, honey, Geoff and his security team were on top of it," Robert jumped in.

"Thank you, Geoff," Denise responded, feeling somewhat relieved to know that a threat to the family had been neutralized so quickly.

"Don't thank me," Geoff said. "Robert had it pretty well under control by the time I arrived. I can see that he'll do anything for his family." Geoff and Robert didn't go into the details of what had happened so as to keep the family from getting any more nervous about the day ahead. "Let's take an alternative route out of here just to be safe," Geoff suggested.

On the way downstairs, Geoff got on his phone and called someone. "Yes, we had an incident, but everyone is fine," he spoke into the phone. "Alert the president and the security team as to what has happened. Teams are on-site checking everything out, and they'll report to you what they find. We're on the move to your location for the alternative press conference. We'll use Oscar-Foxtrot-Foxtrot-Sierra-India-Tango-Echo as a means for the video interviews."

"An off-site press conference, huh?" Robert said, looking at Geoff inquisitively. "You and the superiors thought of everything, didn't you? Via video means that it will be sent through multiple routing methods to keep our location secret, am I correct?"

"You don't miss a beat, do you, Robert?" Geoff responded.

"As I told you before, I try to see all possible scenarios ahead of time. I just keep most of those possibilities to myself so as not to worry my family or anyone else. That's why I was ready for what happened earlier."

The family exited through a back door to the hotel and got into a vehicle that was different from the one they had been riding in up until then. Robert was sure the change of vehicle was another security measure. Once they left, Denise noticed they were headed away from the White House and asked, "Where are we going, Geoff?"

Before Geoff could answer, Robert said, "Somewhere safe. We're still doing the press conference but via video. Then, we're heading right back to Florida as soon as the press conference is over. Am I right about that, Geoff?"

"You're right again, my friend," Geoff confirmed. "As you've been proving all day today, you really do see all possibilities before they occur. Your family's safety is top priority, so we'll not be exposing you out in public for the time being. I apologize for what happened earlier."

"I don't blame you, Geoff," Robert said. "No matter how hard one tries, not all possibilities can be seen ahead of time. You're taking care of us now, and for now, we're all alive and well and ready to get back down to Florida. I suspect, however, that our flight back there won't take a direct route and that the flight transponders will alternate their signals after each landing. Am I right again?" Robert asked.

Geoff didn't answer but instead simply laughed. He then asked Denise, "How do you live with such a know-it-all?"

"Oh, believe it or not, he admits he doesn't know it all," Denise said with a chuckle.

They reached a hangar near a private airfield and drove inside. "Okay, when it's time for the conference, you'll be using this green-screen stage setup," Geoff explained. "That way, we can display any scene around you, and other people participating in the press conference will see the scene on their end even if you do not see it on yours. They'll only see where they think you are, not where you really are. For now, please relax until the press conference begins. You can watch the conference on this television screen over here and see who is asking you questions. Boy, am I glad none of you wore green today!"

Robert asked, "Can we assume that any outside noises that might give away our location will also be blocked out, Geoff?"

"Outside sounds could give a hint to where we are," Geoff confirmed. "But we'll make sure everything is battened down to help prevent that. It might get warm in here, but safety first." Geoff glanced down at his phone. "Okay, I just got notification that the president is heading to the podium. Robert, you and your family get seated." Once the MacMurchaids were all seated, Geoff turned on the monitor and sound system just in time for them to see the president arrive at the podium.

The president started his speech. "My fellow Americans and fellow citizens of earth, I come before you to make an announcement that will be of great interest to all. Since the dawn of humankind, our people have had an undying need to explore and discover. Unfortunately, history has provided relatively few discoveries and even fewer explorers, but these people and events have helped shape the world over time to what we know today.

"Today, I'm announcing that we're taking the next step in exploration and discovery. But before I make that announcement, let's first realize a few things. With every attempt at discovering something new, there's always risk that comes with it. Some discoveries throughout time have resulted in injury, death, or both, which has been a necessary risk. And some explorers have traveled far from home here on earth, for example, the Vikings. We're still learning about just how far the Vikings traveled from home. Our next step in exploration and discovery goes beyond Earth and, in the spirit of the Vikings, is named the 'Valhalla' mission.

"The United States has chosen an exceptional group of individuals to participate in this new mission. These individuals are all part of the same nuclear family. And they'll be all humankind's family when they're soon sent into space. Please look to the viewing screen as I introduce the entire world to the MacMurchaid family." The president motioned to the family on the screen and then led the press room in applause. The MacMurchaids waved to the camera and thus to the world.

The president continued. "The Valhalla mission will take this family to the International Space Station for a period of months. The space station is in space and thus the heavens, which is why the mission is called Valhalla, which has widely become known as the Viking version of heaven. This is a nod to the MacMurchaids' hometown, which is home to a Viking runestone, showing just how far the Vikings went in their own explorations.

"While on the space station, the MacMurchaid family will be closely monitored, and they'll occasionally do experiments that will be suggested by school children and teachers here on Earth. The MacMurchaid children will be our new heroes of exploration and discovery as they show us how to work together and learn in space the way our adult astronauts have done in the past.

"I will now hand this conference over to Robert MacMurchaid, husband to Denise and father to Kris, Tony, Troy, and Nicole. Please hold your questions until later as I know he would like to speak to the world first." The president clapped and stepped back from the podium while Robert stood to speak from the family's secure location.

"Thank you, Mister President," Robert began. "On behalf of the MacMurchaid family, we're honored to be chosen as Earth's first space family. Yes, we're somewhat nervous to go on this mission, as going to space will bring us far out of our comfort zones. As the president noted, we'll be in space for a number of months and, though we'll be busy that entire time, when we're less busy, we'll likely be looking back at Earth, wishing we were back on terra firma with all of you.

"I know there might be questions as to why we agreed to do this. Well, it was my family that submitted the idea of sending an entire family into space to the Universal Space Agency for consideration to begin with. Denise and I grew up during the space race for the moon. And our children have closely followed as many space missions as they could since they were little. And we've all enjoyed space-related sci-fi TV shows and movies throughout our lives. My family even called me 'star child' and later 'mister Spock' when I was growing up. So, this was a hard opportunity to pass up.

"But back to the mission itself and its name. We live in an Oklahoma town by the name of Heavener. On a hill near the town is a large stone, known as the Heavener Runestone, with Viking runes on it, which have been translated and retranslated. Originally, there was also a smaller runestone found near Poteau, Oklahoma, by boys on a class field trip. My wife's older sister was on that field trip, too. So, within a short distance, two runes were found. Others have been found in Oklahoma as well. Since these stones came from Viking explorers who traveled far from home, it seemed natural for our mission to be named after the Vikings.

"My family is also doing this to honor all those who have gone before us, but especially humankind's shared ancestors. There are explorers and discoverers in our ancestral lineage. Whether they came from Eurasia or Africa, they explored the lands around them and made discoveries that enlarged the world they knew. Even those who were the first people of the western hemisphere are of our ancestral lineage. They came to a new place—one with animals, birds, and other things that they had never seen before. We know them through teachings as Native Americans, but many of them prefer to be known as the First People. So, exploring and discovering is in humankind's nature. To deny it would be denying a portion of ourselves and denying our ancestry.

"I think I've spoken enough for now. So, I will now hand things back over to you, Mister President." Robert finished and sat back down.

"Thank you, Robert," the president said, taking over again. "I'm amazed each time I listen to you or the members of your family as you're all filled with wisdom. We can all be confident in the family we've chosen for this mission."

"Thank you, sir, for that compliment," Robert responded. "I know I can speak for the entire MacMurchaid family in saying that I'm forever a student, and, as such, I must also be forever a teacher. I've always felt the need to pass along the information I learn to others."

"Thank you for proving my point about you yet again, Robert," the president said. "We can all be confident in you. I'm going to continue here with the media, but I'll let you and your family go for now since you have a lot of preparation ahead of you for your mission as our first family in space. The media and I will see you later. Until we meet again!"

The press began shouting out questions to the MacMurchaids, but the MacMurchaids waved goodbye as the camera that was on them turned off. The president continued to address the press. "As I said to the MacMurchaid family, you all will have a chance to talk to them and ask questions later. But for now, they're on their way to prepare for their destiny in space. Now, I'd be glad to answer whatever questions I can for a short while."

With that last statement from the president, the monitor the MacMurchaids were watching from the hangar shut off. Geoff then waved the family toward their aircraft, saying, "We have a long series of flights to get you back to the Universal Space Center." With that, everyone boarded a waiting jet and took their seats. Within a short time, they were in the air and headed back to Florida.

Chapter 8

Preparation and Training

THE MACMURCHAID FAMILY arrived back at the Universal Space Center without incident. They were loaded into a vehicle and taken to a building where they would be housed during their time at the center. "Get some rest tonight, for tomorrow starts the beginning of your preparations," Geoff advised everyone. "Training won't begin for another couple of days. But tomorrow, you'll be measured for your space gear and have molds made for your seats for the flight to the space station and your seats on Valkyrie, which is the ship taking you all the way to the moon." Geoff then bid everyone goodnight.

Once their dear friend Geoff had departed, the MacMurchaids settled into what would be their new home for the next couple of months. They quickly fell into their routine of eating an evening meal together, bathing, and getting ready for bed. "I don't know if they'll be keeping us on an early morning schedule or not," Robert pondered out loud. "So, I suggest that everyone try to get as much rest as possible tonight and not try to stay up late. I don't want this to be like at home, where I have difficulty getting you up for school sometimes! Understood?"

"Yes, Daddy, sir," Troy responded while saluting him. The rest of the children nodded their agreement and saluted Robert as well.

"Enough of that, you hellions," Robert jokingly chided them. He then gave each of them a goodnight hug before they headed to bed.

Denise and Robert finally had some alone time to sit and talk privately. "Robert, what was that all about earlier today? I mean, the deal with the man coming to the door of our suite and then us not being seated near the president for the press conference?" Denise tried not to look worried as she asked.

"There was a small breach of security that necessitated a last-minute change in protocol. With all the craziness in the world today from different groups and factions, it's not that surprising that something like this happened. But I didn't think it would happen before we were even announced to the world. We might never be informed who the guy actually was or if he was acting alone. They don't want us worried about that kind of thing. And now that we've been announced to the world and are at this facility, we have more stringent security and protocols, so please don't worry, Denise," Robert reassured her.

"But how did you know that man was up to no good?"

"Honey, let's just say that I was prepared to protect my family and leave it at that. Let the details remain with those whose job it is to manage those situations and facts. You and I just need to relax before they train our butts off." Robert kissed

Denise and then escorted her to their bed.

* * *

The next morning, the family's breakfast was brought to them as they were going about their normal morning routines. One of the men who delivered the food said to Robert, "I was ordered to inform you, Captain MacMurchaid, that a detail will be here at 0800 to take you and your family to be fitted for your equipment. Good day, sir." The young man saluted Robert, and Robert saluted back.

"I guess I better get used to that from the younger enlisted people," Robert said, smiling at Denise. "I hope it doesn't become a regular habit during training. I know once the mission is over, I'll be giving and receiving salutes quite regularly."

"Well, you *are* an officer, Robert. But you're also my gentleman." Denise smiled back.

Shortly after everyone ate and had gotten dressed in the special uniforms they had been given on their original flight down from Oklahoma, a knock came from the main door to their suite at precisely 0800. It was Tom. "Good morning, everyone," he said. Everyone said good morning back. "Is everyone ready to be measured, photographed, and molded into astronauts?" Everyone nodded while a couple of the children yawned, having not gone to sleep as early as Robert had recommended. "Good, then let's load up and go to the other end of the base."

As everyone filed out of the suite and toward their waiting vehicle, Tom continued. "Today should be pretty straightforward as far as what you've already been told will occur. But after today, the real training will begin. On the way to your fittings, we'll pass a few of the facilities where some of your training will take place. Some of those facilities house simulations of the space station that we'll use to train you and also to record each of you doing the tasks that you'll later be asked to perform during the Valhalla mission." Everyone got into a waiting vehicle, and the vehicle departed to take them to the other end of the Universal Space Center base.

After arriving at their destination, everyone disembarked from the vehicle, and they were escorted into a building. "Since you can't do all your training in the uniforms you're wearing, you'll each be fitted with uniforms similar to those worn by astronauts during their training," Tom informed the MacMurchaids. "You'll also be fitted for your actual spacesuits, like those that any astronaut wears into space or uses for spacewalks. I don't think any of you will be doing spacewalks, though . . . or at least, I hope not!" Denise seemed unamused by Tom's joke.

"These technicians will measure each of you for your gear," Tom continued. "And they'll assist you in being seated in a molding compound so that your seats on the craft taking you to the space station and your seats on Valkyrie—the craft taking you from the space station to the moon—will be perfectly fitted to each of you. Don't worry; the compound is in a plastic film so that it won't come into contact with you. There is a team assigned to each of you. So, please relax, and let them do their work. The real stuff starts tomorrow."

"Now you've got me wishing I had started weightlifting after Niki was born, as I did in college when Robert and I first met," Denise exclaimed.

"Don't worry, honey," Robert soothed her. "It'll be fine. Besides, you look fine to me! As long as you're healthy, which you are, you'll do fine." Robert smiled toward Denise and blew a kiss to her. By then, they were already being measured by their teams. As Tom headed to the door, Robert asked, "Where are you going now?"

"Some of us work around here, Robert. I need to meet with the members of your training team. We have to go over the schedule and make sure everything is in working order so that we can get you ready for your flight. You'll meet with some of your team tomorrow. Don't worry; I'll be back to check on your progress."

"Okay, but don't be a stranger," Robert responded.

After all the measurements for their suits were complete, the MacMurchaids were escorted by their teams of technicians to another room to be molded and fitted for their seats. "We'll help place you into these molding chairs so that there won't be any abnormal shaping that could cause problems during flight," one of the team members informed the family. "After we set you in the chair, try to be perfectly still for fifteen minutes," he instructed them.

"That might be a problem for these hellions," Denise whispered to Robert, nodding toward their children. "And don't you go to sleep while sitting for so long," she teased him.

"I'll do my best to remain awake," Robert whispered back to her. "It isn't a roller coaster, for goodness' sake." Both of them tried to keep from laughing out loud.

After the family was seated, they did their best to remain

still for the entire fifteen minutes, but time seemed to pass incredibly slowly. Finally, the technicians lifted the family members out of their chairs and escorted them to a dining area to eat lunch. When lunch was over, a technician entered the dining area and asked, "Will you all please follow me?" The family members headed back to the first room, where their measurements had been taken. "We were able to get some fabric cut for your jumpsuits and uniforms. But before we stitch them together, we want to ensure that the cuts we made aren't going to cause problems during the final assembly." The technicians re-measured the family, using almost the same measurements they had taken earlier, but this time using the measuring tapes while also holding sections of their uniforms up to their bodies.

Robert asked, "Is this normal? I mean, is this what all astronauts go through?"

One technician answered, "No, we have standard uniform sizes for the astronauts. But since your mission is a special one and since some of your family members are not adults, we have to ensure everything fits just right. You, sir, are the only one who we might consider a standard uniform size."

"Understood," Robert replied.

After considerable examination of each piece of fabric for each family member, the technicians said they were done and took the family to a new room where they were then seated. "Would you please wait here for Captain Hollett?" a technician asked. Robert nodded to her that they would.

After a brief time, Tom entered the room with two other individuals. "I would like you to meet your instructors who will be with you as you receive your training as I watch from control rooms near each training simulator. They'll also be with you during your mission itself. This young man is Captain Donavan Beltron, who will be the command pilot for your mission." Everyone said hello to Donavan. "And this young lady is Captain Isis LaStarr, who will be the co-pilot for your mission." Everyone said hello to Isis.

Isis responded by saying, "Please call me Izzy."

Then everyone said, "Hello, Izzy."

After all introductions were finished, Tom said, "Like I said, these two are a part of your mission. They'll not only pilot you to the International Space Station but will also pilot the Valkyrie craft to Valhalla on the moon. Once you have been secured in your chambers at Valhalla, they and the technicians we call angels will return to the space station. After your three months at Valhalla are over, they'll return to Valhalla and bring you back to the space station. You'll then return to earth. So basically, all eight of you are members of one team. I wanted you all to meet before you start your training tomorrow."

"I'm glad we'll remain a team throughout the mission," Robert asserted, addressing everyone at once. "It's better than being thrown to one set of astronauts and then passed to another set. As a team, we'll develop trust amongst us."

Donavan responded, "I feel you've hit the nail on the head, Captain MacMurchaid. Izzy and I have worked together before, so we already have that trust. Now, we're looking forward to collaborating with you and your family and building the same trust between all of us."

Izzy stepped in, saying, "Our first day of trust is tomorrow.

Since tomorrow we'll be working on some of the simulators, tomorrow's trust will be built on a simulated flight. So, don't eat a heavy breakfast tomorrow morning!" Izzy warned them with a big grin.

Robert knew exactly what Izzy was talking about. They were going to ride the newer so-called "vomit comet" simulator. And he assumed they might later be using the centrifuge, which would require them to eat light. Since the centrifuge was used to simulate increased gravitational forces during launch, he had heard of some people who were in it for the first time becoming nauseated. He hoped his family would be fine since they had experienced and enjoyed carnival rides many times before. He also thought of some of the crazy stunts his children would attempt with each other and their friends, and he was further confident they would be fine the next day.

Izzy then asked, "Well then, who's ready to get something to eat?"

The children all screamed out in near unison, "Me!"

Denise wasn't as confident as Robert, though. And as they left to go eat, she pulled Robert closer and asked him, "What did she mean about the flight tomorrow?"

Robert leaned close to her and said, "Two words: vomit comet. But before you worry too much, just remember that you do great on airplanes and have been fine on carnival rides."

"That doesn't help much, honey," she replied. "This seems totally different."

"If you don't think about it too much, you'll be fine, honey," Robert assured her. "We just need to remember to control what the kids eat in the morning."

* * *

The next morning, everyone in the family was up bright and early. By now, they were well settled into their new daily routine away from home. But the children noticed that there were not as many choices to eat at breakfast that morning. Nicole asked, "Daddy, why don't we have our usual breakfast items?"

Robert smiled at her and said, "Do you remember what Izzy told us yesterday about not eating a heavy breakfast? Well, today we'll be riding somewhat of a roller-coaster in the sky, you might say. And she doesn't want anyone to get sick."

Nicole had a puzzled look on her face. Troy leaned toward his sister and said, "Dad means the vomit comet, Niki." A great big grin crossed her face as she suddenly understood.

Shortly after everyone finished eating their small breakfasts, there was a knock at the door to their suite. It was Donavan. "We're here to pick you up and start your astronaut training," he informed them. "Is everyone ready?" The kids immediately went to the door, nearly running their mom and dad over in the process. "Okay, good. Let's load up."

After a short ride, they pulled up beside an aircraft. Everyone filed out of the vehicle, and Donavan explained, "This is the newest version of what many people call the 'vomit comet.' It flies just like any other aircraft but can handle sudden climbs and dives better than many others out there. We're going to begin getting you ready for being in space by putting you through several short periods of simulated weightlessness. You'll get used to this ride sooner or later because we'll ride this bird many times before the day of the launch."

Izzy stepped out from the aircraft and said, "Also, if you're good and don't get sick, you'll get to experience a few acrobatics that only a small number of people have ever experienced. So, if everyone is ready, please get on board and buckle in for take-off."

Once they reached their cruising altitude for the beginning of their training, everyone got out of their seats and went to the open area where Donavan and Izzy were ready for them. "Get ready for climbs and dives," Donavan said. He and Izzy then showed the family how to position themselves for the climbs.

After several sessions of weightlessness, the family was instructed to be seated and buckle in again because they were heading back to base. After the aircraft landed and came to a complete stop, everyone unbuckled themselves and waited for the okay to disembark. Once on the tarmac, Izzy asked, "Is everyone okay? And did everyone enjoy themselves?"

The children, answering in near unison as they often did, responded, "Yeah!"

"When can we do it again?" Tony asked Izzy.

Denise cut in, saying, "I'm sure they have us scheduled for a few more trips on this plane. Don't worry. Izzy, it wasn't as bad as I was expecting. Like my children, I'm looking forward to future training sessions."

"Good," Izzy responded. She then asked Robert, "What did *you* think of the ride?"

Robert grinned and said, "Normally, I tend to doze on roller-coasters. But this airborne version was very pleasant. I'd always wanted to experience it ever since I dreamed as a child of being an astronaut. I'm looking forward to more rides like this one."

Donavan stepped in and said, "As a precaution, those in charge want a medical team to check you all out and make sure you don't have any ill effects from the ride. They're being extra cautious since most of you are younger than any astronauts before you."

After the family had their medical checkups, they returned to their quarters. When they arrived, they found Tom standing near the entrance. "Welcome back from your first day of training," he said as he let the family go inside. "Everyone is okay and enjoyed themselves?" Seeing that the answer was yes, he said, "Good! Well, now for the bad news. This was the easiest day of your training." He tried soothing them with a gentle smile. "By that, I mean that over the months-long period before launch, you'll have slow days and you'll have hectic days. The slow days will be more like today, while the hectic days will have each of you spending several hours completing tasks. You're heading into space, and we want you to be as prepared as possible to handle things on your own without much assistance from fully-trained astronauts. They have years of training in their fields and as astronauts. But you'll only have months."

"We've occasionally discussed as a family what astronauts go through during their training," Robert informed Tom. "We have related movies and books and such at home that the children have had the opportunity to view over the years. So, we have a general idea of what is ahead for us even though, in this case, it's under extraordinary circumstances. We know we won't be pushed to the full extent that astronauts are, but we're willing as a family to push as close to that level as we can. Even if some of us might moan and complain along the way, I assure you, we're fully committed to this endeavor."

"I am glad to hear that, Robert. Not every family would have that attitude, which is part of why we chose your family for this mission to begin with. And if this program were not the first and were not on a rushed schedule, you would have more time to become fully-trained astronauts instead of simply astronaut-trained passengers aboard the space station," Tom explained. "I've received word that your launch has been scheduled for January. I suspect they hope to launch you on New Year's Day as a special event."

"That means our training will have to come to an end in December," Denise realized out loud. "We'll try to be ready."

"I hope the powers that be don't plan on parading us around at events anytime soon. The training we need for this endeavor won't allow for that," Robert cautioned. "Any interviews we're expected to have between now and then, I expect them to be held here at the base, whether in person or on video. That's how much my family and I are committed to this. My family will not take part in a dog and pony show. I hope I've made myself understood, Tom, my friend."

"I expected nothing less from you, Robert. I already informed those who might want to parade your family around that this would be how you felt. And now, you've told them yourself, via videoconference." Tom pointed to a camera mounted from the ceiling.

"You could have warned us," Robert said, feeling sheepish. He then turned to the camera and said, "As you just heard me explain to Captain Hollett, this is how serious my family and I feel about this mission. If you want a family to parade around for media events, you chose the wrong family. When we commit to something, either as individuals or as a family, we *stay* committed. We know there's a lot of work ahead of us in our training, and we do not expect it to be easy. In fact, I feel that each of us will at some point during our training be asking for even more training than what has been planned because that's how Denise and I approach things, and that's how we brought up our children. We have a strong work ethic. If I've upset any of you by what I just said, then maybe this mission should be postponed until you find a family that's willing to be full-fledged puppets. I don't apologize for how I feel about that."

The clapping of one pair of hands could be heard on the audio feed from the monitor near the family. "I said before that you're an honest man, Captain MacMurchaid," came the president's voice. He finished clapping, then said, "And I had a feeling that you were strongly committed to this mission when you spoke at our dinner question-and-answer session. Now, I know for sure that I'm right about you. Don't worry; I'll back you on your feelings about parading your family around. I like your spunk and how committed your entire family is toward your mission. You'll get the training you need, and if that means postponing the launch until you do, then so be it. Your family is what this country needs for inspiration on many levels. We'll explain to the world your commitment and show videos of you and your family training along the way. As for the interviews, we'll handle those as time permits and only on video."

Robert was shocked to hear the president's voice. He responded, "If I may, sir, my personal observation of some of those around you at our dinner would indicate that some of them did not like my attitude, some did not like my statements, and a few of them wanted to control my family and me like we're puppets. I could be wrong in my observations, but that is what I feel even now. Maybe they would even want me court-martialed for insubordination since I'm a USAF officer again."

As Robert was speaking, the president scanned the faces of the officers and government officials sitting around him. Once Robert had finished, the president said, "You know, my boy, you might be right in your observations because I'm seeing pretty much the same thing right now, as we speak. We'll deal with them later. For now, I'm giving the order that your family's mission is to remain on track, and it has my full backing and support. Good day, MacMurchaids." With that, the monitor and the camera shut off.

"Well, I think this has been a very full day of training," Tom said in a cheery tone, trying to lighten the mood.

"Yes. And some of it unexpected," Denise said. "I don't know about you kids, but I'm sure proud of your father for standing his ground despite the possible consequences. What do you feel?"

"Yeah, Dad!" Tony agreed.

"You the man, Dad!" Troy chimed in.

"All right, Daddy! Kris added.

The children had never seen their dad speak so sternly about anything like that before, and they were somewhat surprised. Tom added to their excitement by saying, "After a show like that and after your light breakfast this morning, I think I'll order a pizza party for the MacMurchaid family tonight." The children started jumping for joy while Robert and Denise just smiled at each other. "Just remember, though, that you're on a training schedule. So, get plenty of rest tonight, and I will see you in the morning." With that, Tom exited the door, leaving the family to itself.

As the MacMurchaids were warned, their months of training did involve many hectic days. And as Robert had told Donavan and Izzy, his family did indeed want to learn more than just what was involved with their regularly scheduled training. As the training progressed, tasks were added in relation to each family member's specific interests. With the extra training, they were progressing ahead of the schedule that had been set forth by the powers that be. The MacMurchaids were trying to take in all they could because to them, their mission went beyond them simply being passengers and test subjects. As far as they were concerned, they were becoming an actual part of the crews they would be in contact with throughout their mission. And as such, they wanted to be able to assist their fellow crewmembers with possible tasks that might arise.

As the holidays approached, Tom came to the family one day and said, "Since the holidays are here and you're already way ahead of the curve, we're going to ease back on the training between now and the launch date. You'll still train on certain things, but you're already well prepared for the launch itself. There's been mention but no official confirmation yet that your liftoff could be moved up. And since we're starting to ease your training, we figured it would be nice if your families back in Oklahoma were brought here to spend Thanksgiving with you."

"Thank you! That would be great, wouldn't it, kids?" Denise asked the children.

The children responded with various versions of, "Yeah!"

So, the MacMurchaids were able to finally spend time with their families from back home before they spent months in space. Up until then, they had only spoken with or seen their other family members on phone calls, video calls, and recorded video messages. This would definitely be a memorable Thanksgiving for all. They were all truly thankful on that Thanksgiving Day!

Chapter 9

The Mission Begins

THE RUMORS OF A moved-up launch date that Tom had mentioned prior to Thanksgiving were confirmed, and the new plan was to have the MacMurchaids on the space station before Christmas Day. As the new launch date approached, the family did a few interviews with a select few reporters from various news agencies. For security reasons, the interviews were held in secure rooms because no one had forgotten about the incident in Washington earlier in the year. The reporters were the only news agency members allowed in the room with the MacMurchaids. The personnel who operated the cameras and other recording equipment were employees of the Universal Space Agency. Even the equipment used belonged to the space agency. It was clear that the powers that be were not taking anything lightly.

The interviews ceased days before the launch. And the MacMurchaids were able to spend time with their family, their crew, and the friends they had made over the prior months in more of a family-like atmosphere than a training atmosphere.

In fact, their crew and friends had arranged an early Christmas for the MacMurchaids since they would be spending Christmas Day on the space station. Everyone enjoyed themselves at the celebration as though it were the real holiday.

The day of the launch started pretty much like any other day for the MacMurchaids except for them having to awaken earlier than usual and don their spacesuits. They were eventually taken to the launchpad to ride the elevator up to their waiting spacecraft, and they were then strapped into their seats. The family listened to the communications between launch control, Captain Beltron, and Captain LaStarr as the countdown was underway. Everyone was hoping there would not be any holds in the countdown and that lift-off would occur exactly as planned, at 2:50 p.m. eastern time and 1:50 p.m. central time.

Luckily, everything proceeded as planned. The weather was favorable, and the final countdown was happening. The family could feel when the main engine started. Then, they watched the windows so they could see when they were lifting off. Over the communications system, they heard, "They have cleared the tower." The MacMurchaids knew this meant that any decisions from then on would come from mission control unless Captain Beltron used the abort switch. They were starting to feel the increased g-forces on them as the spacecraft climbed and throttle-up was ordered. They watched as the sky went from the blue of Earth's atmosphere to the blackness of space. They all thought to themselves how different it was viewing this in person than watching it on television or in movies.

The family all noticed when the separation of stage one

and the engine start of stage two occurred. Then, once stage two had shut down, Izzy turned to the family and said, "You can take your helmets off and get out of your seats now. It will be some time before we get close to the space station. Go ahead and look out the windows to enjoy the views!"

Each family member got out of their seat, with the older boys helping their siblings. Then, they floated over to the view ports and got their first personal view of Earth from space. After a few moments of silence, Denise finally said, "It's beautiful. What we've seen in photos, through television, and in videos and movies did not do what I'm seeing here justice." She and Robert put their arms around each other as best they could, though it was difficult since they were still in their spacesuits.

"Wow," "Golly," "Pretty," "Magnificent" were a few of the words the children used to describe what they were seeing.

Donavan told the family, "A few more maneuvers before getting to the space station, and you'll then have a clear view of the moon. It's something to behold without the distortion of Earth's atmosphere. Make sure you store your gear so that it won't be floating into anything."

After circling Earth for a while, they could finally see that they were coming into range of the International Space Station. "Wow! It's a lot bigger in person than I imagined it from the descriptions and pictures I've seen," Troy stated.

The whole family was in awe of what they were seeing and experiencing. All the training they received could not have prepared them emotionally for this. Intellectually, they were prepared. But with every passing minute since liftoff, they realized they had been unprepared emotionally. They knew they were ready for this, but since this was all new for them, there was that part of them that was in every human being asking, *Am I really ready for this, and am I up to the task?* Countless well-known historical figures had undoubtedly asked themselves those same questions or similar questions throughout history. And now, the MacMurchaids were making history. They were *living* history.

After a few maneuvers, the spacecraft docked to the space station. A brief time later, the hatch between the craft and the space station opened, and the family and crew were welcomed by the crew members already living at the station. Everyone shook hands and posed for the cameras that were feeding their arrival back to people on Earth.

"Welcome to your home for the next few months," Tom told the MacMurchaids, speaking from mission control back on Earth. "You might be surprised by the number of people here on Earth that are celebrating your arrival. This mission has already been a massive success so far. Once you've settled in there, there will be a press conference that will include the president. I'll talk to you more after that. For now, I'm glad you made it aboard safely!"

Everybody waved goodbye to Tom. Then, after about thirty minutes, they all gathered in one of the main sections of the space station to await the signal that the press conference was ready to begin. They did not have to wait long before the monitor they were watching showed the White House briefing room. "Ladies and gentlemen, the president of the United States of America," a lady at the podium announced before stepping away from it.

The president walked up to the podium and began to speak. "Greetings, my fellow Americans and citizens of Earth. You were able to watch the launch of our first entire family to travel to space. And you can now see them aboard the International Space Station." With that, the monitor next to the president showed everyone on the station. "Greetings to all of you up there," he said. Everyone waved to the president and to the people of Earth. "First, let me say that the launch was an exciting event to watch. I'm now excited to speak with you and with the crew of the space station. How is your experience so far?"

Robert spoke first. "I think I'll let the children say how we feel since they seem to convey it better than we adults might."

Kris said, "It's awesome so far."

Tony said, "It's been one heck of a ride."

Next, Troy, saying, "The ride up here was great. But the views are even better!"

And finally, Nicole said, "Earth is so pretty from up here. It looks better than any picture I've ever seen of it."

The president responded, "Captain MacMurchaid, I think you're correct. They do express it better than most adults would. I look forward to hearing more from them as your mission continues. I see your wonderful wife there as well. Let's hear from her, please?"

Denise said, "Like Robert and you say, our children can tell you more about how we feel all the way up here than I could express myself. But it's very exciting, and I hope we're worthy to be the first of many families to begin traveling into space."

"I assure you, your family has proven that you're all worthy since the first day you agreed to this adventure," the president stated. "Having received updates from your training to now, I've been continually impressed with how well your family has done. For some of us, your family has exceeded our wildest expectations."

"Thank you, sir," Robert responded on behalf of the entire family.

"Captain Beltron and Captain LaStarr, how do you think your crewmates are doing so far?" the president asked.

Captain Beltron responded first. "Like you said, they're exceeding expectations."

Captain LaStarr then added, "They've handled everything thrown at them during training and the flight here with flying colors."

The president asked the crew of the space station, "So, what does the crew of the International Space Station think about these guests they'll have aboard for the next several months?"

The lead space station crewmember responded, "They're not what we expected, and I mean that in a good way. They already demonstrate great knowledge of how things are done up here. The children are well-mannered, and they show all of us respect, which we also did not expect. I think the next several months will be very interesting and educational for all of us, sir."

"That's good to hear," the president said. "I'll now hand this over to Congressman Pitts." He stepped back and shook Geoff's hand before leaving the room.

Geoff then spoke. "First of all, your family members back in Oklahoma wanted me to tell you that they're extremely proud of what you've accomplished so far. They also send their love."

With that, Robert interjected, "From us to them and to you, our family sends its love as well. And to the people of Earth, we share that love with you, too."

"Thank you, Robert." Geoff continued by saying, "A press release will be given to each of you in this room and sent to news agencies around the world. In that release will be the MacMurchaids' schedule for the next several months on the space station. At the end of their time there, they'll return home to Earth and rest for a while before they'll be allowed to travel for interviews. We here in Washington wish the MacMurchaids and their crewmates God's speed as you soar through the heavens above us."

With that, everyone on the space station waved goodbye before the cameras and the monitor showing them to the people of Earth shut off. "I'm glad they didn't do a question-and-answer session because we have plenty to deal with without all that," Robert said. Everyone nodded or voiced their agreement with what he said.

Over the next couple of months, the family was extremely busy on the space station. They were videoed exercising, sleeping, and conducting activities pretty much every single day. The idea was for these videos to be played back to the people of Earth so that they would believe the family was still on the space station when, in reality, the family would be on their real mission—traveling to Valhalla on the moon, going into pseudo-death there, then returning to the space station. The videos would provide the perfect cover.

With everyone so busy, the months aboard the space station passed quickly. The time for the MacMurchaids to board the Valkyrie spacecraft and ride to Valhalla on the moon was fast approaching.

Chapter 10

Flight to the Moon

THE DAY ARRIVED for the MacMurchaids to load into the Valkyrie spacecraft along with everything they would need for their mission. Kris decided to ask Donavan a question: "How are we supposed to hide the fact that we're leaving?"

Donavan answered by saying, "Valkyrie has remained hidden by the space station so far. The station will be in line with the moon when we depart, so it will hide our departure from people on Earth. It has been arranged for a space anomaly, or "glitch," to happen with all satellites, including ours, when we fire our thrusters. This glitch will allow us to start our travel undetected. The glitch will disappear as suddenly as it came. We'll only use thrust burst to keep us going and then make any course corrections as we need them. When we're near the moon, we can then use the thrusters to slow us down and help us land at Valhalla. Okay?"

"I trust you that it will work," Kris responded. "But at this point, I guess we have no choice. We'll just have to see. Will it take us the same amount of time to get to the moon as it took the Apollo missions?" he asked.

This time Izzy answered. "We'll arrive a little faster since we'll be doing multiple short thruster bursts on the way there. Those bursts will increase our speed for getting there. That wasn't available during the Apollo missions."

"I remember hearing about that during training now," Kris responded.

"Okay, all those going to Valhalla, get inside and buckle in," Donavan announced. "This has to be timed perfectly for us not to be noticed."

Tony was the next to ask a question. "Even with all the precautions you just told Kris about, won't the ship be seen?"

Robert answered this one. "If either of you had paid attention during our training briefings, you would know that they already explained things to us. The ship is colored to match space debris or space rocks. It also has a radar image similar to those things. There will be no radio signal from it to give us away except when scheduled or necessary. Now buckle up and enjoy the ride."

With that, the rest of the family got into Valkyrie, sat themselves, and buckled in. Everyone watched the countdown clock overhead between the pilot's and co-pilot's seats as it counted down to departure. When it reached zero, there was a brief thruster fire, and then they were on their way to the moon.

The flight went pretty much as planned, and the family watched as Earth gradually seemed to get smaller behind them and the moon seemed to grow ahead of them. They knew they would be at Valhalla soon. And from what they were told, the main entrance to their station there would be in the side of the Jules Verne Crater.

Creating Valhalla had been made easier when the team excavating for the station discovered what appeared to be a cave on the side of the crater. Later investigation revealed that the cave had been created by a partial collapse of the crater wall in that location. The only thing that kept the wall from completely falling down and covering the hole was a strong, thick layer of basalt holding up the upper wall of the crater. The MacMurchaids were not told how long it took to build Valhalla or to place the well-camouflaged sensors and equipment they needed in the surrounding area. All that mattered to the forward-looking MacMurchaids anyway was that this was where they would be spending the next three months.

After what seemed like a long flight, the family and their pilots finally began the slowdown process as they neared the moon. The family looked on in amazement at how big the moon was—much bigger, of course, than it appeared to them when standing on Earth. Yes, they knew how big it was from their knowledge of the Apollo missions and satellite images, but it was an enormous difference being there and seeing it in person.

The pilots began to take the spacecraft toward the dark side of the moon. Instead of having to do as the astronauts did during the moon landings, on this trip, they were going to be landing like they did in science fiction movies and television shows. Donavan announced, "We're now on final approach. Ahead of us is the Jules Verne Crater and Valhalla. Get seated and buckle in for landing."

The family did as they were told, and Donavan eased Valkyrie into the crater until they were in front of a large blast door, which Robert figured must lead into Valhalla. The door opened fully, and Donavan piloted the ship into the area between that door and another door. Once the ship touched down in that area, the outer door closed and sealed. Then, the inner door slowly began to open. Once it was fully open, Valkyrie maneuvered inside to a marked landing site.

Donavan set Valkyrie down on the landing site and shut its engines off as the inner door shut behind them. "We've reached our destination," Donavan informed everyone as he unbuckled from his seat. "Welcome to Valhalla!"

Chapter 11

Valhalla

AS EVERYONE GOT UP, the hatch on the side of Valkyrie opened, and a technician climbed the steps coming in. He said, "Welcome to Valhalla. This will be your home away from home for the next three months." The technician helped everyone out of the ship and onto the floor of Valkyrie's hangar. "Don't worry about your gear. Some of the other technicians will unload it and place it in storage. We'll be your angels while you're here."

"Angels?!" Nicole looked at the man with a puzzled look on her face, having forgotten that this term had been explained to her family during training.

"Yes, that's how we're known to Odin, which is the name of the computer that runs this place," the technician responded. "We still go by our names amongst ourselves, but when Odin speaks to one of us, he calls us Angel, followed by a designated number. As for you, you'll be known as 'Subjects' along with designated call numbers until there eventually comes a time when Odin will call you by name. We'll have introductions here in a while, in the dining area. Until then, you can be seated in that area until the angels finish their tasks."

The technician offered a quick tour of the facility on the level the family came into. "This facility has many levels dug into the lunar crust. Some levels are there for safety reasons, such as fuel storage and radiation protection from the miniature nuclear processor. Other levels are for storage of supplies. Odin himself, or should I say his primary memory core, is deep under the surface. This facility might be awe-inspiring for you to look at, but to us who spend time here, it's just our lunar home until we head back to our Terran home."

"It's definitely big," Nicole noted out loud.

"What do you mean 'big?' It's *huge!*" Troy corrected his sister.

Each family member had their own thoughts and comments about Valhalla as the tour continued back toward the main hangar area. Eventually, the technician escorted the family to the dining area and let them be seated. Within a brief time, they were joined by all the rest of the technicians, along with Donavan and Izzy.

Donavan said, "These folks here will give you a medical checkup to make sure you're fine from your trip here. They'll also assist each of you when you enter your chambers for your three-month sleep in Loki's Breath. Once you're asleep, we'll monitor you for a short while before we turn your monitoring over to Odin and return to the space station. Odin has been programmed as to what information to feed each of you while you're in hibernation, as well as to monitor all your vitals.

"While in hibernation," Donavan continued, "your bodies

will still function but at an extremely decreased rate. Odin can detect any details concerning each of you through the nano-pulses your bodies will still be giving off. He'll relay those details back to the space station. In three months, this group will return to help awaken you and assist you out of your chambers. You'll then be given physical examinations before your return to the space station. The technicians will stay here during your return to the station, and you'll spend the rest of your mission at the station until we return to Earth in the same craft you originally arrived on. Any questions?"

There was some discussion amongst the family members, but they did not voice any concerns. They were then given protein meals and drinks before they were taken to get physicals. While they consumed the meals and drinks, the technicians individually introduced themselves to the family and let them know they had been watching and reading about the MacMurchaids since their very first press conference. The technicians let the family know that they considered them all full-fledged members of the space agency family and that they were honored to have finally met them in person.

"I'm Angel One, but my real name is Spencer Reasoning. I hope once the mission is over that you'll still be involved with the space agency."

"I'm Angel Three, but my name is Dilan McDonald. And this is my brother, Angel Two, better known as Jordan McDonald. We share Spencer's feelings."

"I'm Angel Four, but everyone calls me Abby. It's short for Abbigayle Faithe. Hopefully, we can have get-togethers with you in the future."

The rest of the technicians introduced themselves as well, and everyone had a chance to talk with each other before getting down to business.

Chapter 12

Time to Sleep

AFTER THE MACMURCHAIDS finished their meals, they were escorted to another room and each given clothing and a helmet to wear while they would be in the Loki's Breath chambers. They were then given their physicals and escorted to their individual chambers. Before they were completely in their chambers, the technicians attached monitor leads to their bodies to aid in Odin's ability to monitor each family member. Then, the family members were all asked to lay down and get relaxed. After they were all in position, their chambers were closed.

Izzy then told them, "Just breathe normally. Loki's Breath does not have a smell, and you'll basically fall asleep." Each family member did their best to remain calm and relaxed. And they did not even realize when Loki's Breath began entering their chambers. Soon, the entire family was in pseudo-death hibernation. Izzy then turned to Donavan and said, "They're all under. All vitals are going to the levels expected. The chambers appear to be functioning as they should."

"Good," Donavan responded. "I didn't want to tell them, but our departure time from Valhalla has been moved up. So, we can only stay a couple of hours instead of a couple of days like originally planned."

Izzy and the technicians were shocked. "What?!" Izzy exclaimed.

"Don't worry; Odin will take over monitoring immediately," Donavan explained. "We've been ordered back to the space station and must comply. Once we leave, Odin will fill the entire facility with Loki's Breath. Apparently, bad things are happening back on earth, and mission control wants us safe on the station. They've already ordered the station crew to empty all supply crafts and crew crafts of all nonessential items to prepare the crafts in case they're needed to transport everyone back to Earth."

"What about the family we just put into pseudo-death sleep chambers?" Izzy asked. "Are we going to awaken them or just leave them here? This isn't right!" she protested.

"Those in charge feel that since few people know about this part of the mission or Valhalla, that our new friends will be safer here," Donavan continued. "We have our orders, and Odin will be in complete charge once we leave. So, load up people. There's no time to waste."

To the extent that time allowed, everyone did what they were required to do before leaving Valhalla, and then they gathered at Valkyrie prior to boarding. Donavan told everyone to get in and buckle up for launch. After the hatch was sealed, he got into his commander's seat and buckled in. "Odin, open Valkyrie hangar inner door."

"AFFIRMATIVE," came Odin's voice across the ship's intercom as the door began its opening process.

Once the inner door was fully open, Donavan maneuvered Valkyrie in-between the inner and outer doors. He then said, "Odin, close inner door."

"AFFIRMATIVE."

Once the inner door was closed and sealed, Donavan commanded Odin to open the outer door, and Odin complied. Once the outer door was open, Valkyrie lifted off and headed out of Valhalla and up out of the crater. Valkyrie hovered above the crater for a few moments while Donavan gave Odin his final commands prior to leaving. "Odin, close the outer door and seal Valhalla until the angels return. Understood?"

"AFFIRMATIVE." Odin did as he was told, and Valkyrie began its trip back to the space station. Donavan and Izzy made thruster adjustments along the way to leave the moon behind.

"We're on our way to the space station; settle in for the ride," Donavan told everyone. "We'll be heading back a bit quicker than we have before so that we can be at the station when mission control wants us there." As they left the moon behind, he thought to himself, *Good luck, MacMurchaids, my friends. You're in a safer place than the home you left behind.*

Chapter 13

War Begins

AS VALKYRIE NEARED the International Space Station, its crew and passengers monitored audio feeds that were covering attacks happening in various places on Earth. Most of the attacks were being carried out by small groups of masked, armed men or small militias with military-grade arms and explosives. But so far, there was no mention of attacks on embassies or military posts. What was still unclear to everyone was who was carrying out the attacks since no country or faction had yet claimed responsibility.

"Okay, once Captain Beltron docks Valkyrie and the hatch is safe to open, everyone needs to help make sure the station crew has made room in all the capsules for personnel returning to earth," Izzy explained to the technicians. "We need to be ready for orders from mission control if they want all of us off the space station."

Everyone on board indicated that they understood the tasks ahead of them. They knew they would be briefed on the reasoning behind all of this later on, when they had the need to know from the ranking officials. Meanwhile, Valkyrie was maneuvered into docking position and was able to get a hard dock with the station. Soon, the hatch leading into the space station was opened, and everyone got busy with preparations.

It did not take long for the capsules to be cleared since a lot of the work had already been started by the space station crew. Everyone was assigned to a capsule they would board, and they all assembled in an area near the capsules. The only people who did not gather there were the crew members who could make course corrections for the space station—Donavan and Izzy.

After waiting for what seemed to be an eternity, the space station received word from mission control that some debris appeared to have bumped them from their usual orbit and that they would need to make a course correction. The crew began the course correction, but Donavan noticed something odd on the space station's radar. "Izzy, look at this and tell me if you see what I see."

Izzy arrived at the radar station and watched the blips on the screen. "Hold on a minute! Those appear to be adjusting course to match with the station as if being guided into a collision course with us!"

"That's what it looks like to me as well," Donavan confirmed. Then, as they continued watching the radar, new blips began appearing from separate locations but all heading toward the station. Donavan then sounded the alarm, "All personnel abandon the station!" he instructed over the intercom. "I repeat, all personnel aboard the station, we are under attack. Abandon ship."

Donavan then signaled the flight crew to leave as well while he and Izzy programmed a course maneuver into the guidance computer. "There! That should have the station maneuvering as if it were trying to avoid a collision, which should allow the capsules to return to Earth safely," Izzy said. Donavan and Izzy nodded at each other and then left the controls. Since all the capsules had left before Donavan and Izzy could board one, they had no choice but to board Valkyrie instead.

Once Donavan and Izzy were inside Valkyrie and buckled in, they undocked the spacecraft. "You know we're going to have to do controlled maneuvers to safely enter Earth's atmosphere and land, right?" Izzy pointed out. "Valkyrie was mainly designed to stay in space."

Donavan glanced at Izzy and said, "Well, if any team can do the seemingly impossible task of piloting this space craft back to Earth, I believe it's us. I'm glad you're my co-pilot." Izzy nodded in agreement, and Donavan continued. "I figure we'll have to come at the atmosphere very shallow since we don't have the usual heat shields. Luckily, the alloy that the skin and structure are made from can withstand elevated temperatures. We'll basically be burping the thrusters to keep us from bouncing off the atmosphere and to ease us down into it. We'll keep doing it until we're well within the atmosphere and then let gravity take over. We'll still keep ourselves in a very shallow dive, though, and make turns every so often to help shed any heat buildup. Once we're down to a decent flight level, we'll use the thrusters to help us get to the nearest landing base or a navy carrier. Are you ready, Izzy?"

"Let's do this!" she confirmed. "You know, if this works, they'll probably call it the Beltron maneuver," Izzy suggested.

Donavan responded, "If it works, I'll insist that we both get credit since it will take both of us to do it. The Beltron-LaStarr maneuver?" They both grinned as they worked the controls together to get back home. They took one more glance back at the station to see if the objects missed it or if they had been right to evacuate. "Izzy, can you put an external camera on automatic to keep a view of the station? I think I saw something that the brass will want to see if we make it through this."

Izzy did as Donavan instructed while doing her best to aid in controlling their descent. Before they got too far into Earth's atmosphere to see the space station, they both noticed flashes coming from the station's direction. They were too busy to tell for sure whether the flashes were explosions. They were getting into the thicker air they needed for surviving their descent back to Earth. They could feel the buffeting from the air going around Valkyrie as they got lower in altitude.

Finally, things began to smooth out, and Donavan and Izzy began to use the thrusters to keep them aloft until they found a place to land. Luckily for them, they could tell they were close to Houston, which was good. But the fuel for the thrusters was getting extremely low since they didn't have time for the tanks to be refilled while at the space station. Donavan and Izzy eventually made it to the Universal Space Agency base in Florida and were in hover mode prior to final landing, at which point the thrusters quit because they had run out of fuel. So, Valkyrie dropped the final eight inches to the ground. But it had landed.

The base's emergency crews and military police headed out to where the unexpected craft had landed. They did not have the need to know before now of Valkyrie's existence. However, Tom had been watching the approach and had a team with him that was ready to beat the responders to Valkyrie. Since he was in uniform, he began issuing orders for the MPs to stand down and for the fire equipment not to spray down the craft. His team members waited for the hatch to open to see who would exit.

Once Donavan and Izzy were out, they explained to Tom and his team that they might want to shuttle Valkyrie into a hangar and download all of its data and video. In response, a member of Tom's team got on the radio and called for a lift to come get the craft off the tarmac and into a secure hangar. After the team loaded Captain Beltron and Captain LaStarr into a waiting vehicle, Captain Hollett got in and welcomed the two home. There were no discussions during the ride back to a secure area. Some things Tom already knew, but not everyone on this ride was privileged to that information.

Once in a secure room in a secure building, Tom had Donavan and Izzy sit down next to a table. He began speaking to them. "We all know that there will be an investigation followed by a review board. But first, I would like to hear directly from you what happened up there."

Donavan began. "While at Valhalla, we received orders to return to the space station earlier than scheduled due to escalating events on Earth. The MacMurchaids are, to our knowledge, currently in pseudo-death at Valhalla, with Odin monitoring them. During our return to the space station, we heard that word had been given for the station crew to prepare all capsules for their personnel and our personnel for possible use in returning to Earth. Once we arrived there, our personnel helped finish preparing the capsules while we helped the flight control personnel prepare for any space station course corrections. Some debris appeared to be floating into the station's orbital path. The station's course was adjusted, but then the debris adjusted its course to match."

As Donavan stopped to take a drink of water, Izzy took over. "We noticed the change in direction from what we thought was debris, and we picked up more of the objects coming at the space station from multiple directions. The order was given by Captain Beltron to abandon the station. He and I programmed in multiple course corrections to make it appear that the space station still had personnel on board controlling it so that the capsules would have time to depart safely."

Izzy paused and took a deep breath before continuing. "Unfortunately, all capsules left before Captain Beltron and I could board one of them. So, we, as a team, decided that even though there was a very slim chance of success, we would take our chances at surviving reentry on Valkyrie. It was our only chance at survival. We had external cameras on Valkyrie watch the space station as we attempted reentry. Through our combined effort and a ship that was well built, we made it back here safely."

Donavan stopped her there and resumed speaking to Tom. "Those were no ordinary pieces of debris, if they were debris at all. They all made course corrections, sir. Right before we entered Earth's upper atmosphere, it appeared to me as though there were small bursts from the rear of those items, like miniature thrusters. Hopefully, data sent back from the space station and the data from Valkyrie will help us find out what truly happened."

Tom looked at both of them and said, "Just before the space station was destroyed, something began blocking any signals from it. Some of what you told me did get through to us, and we do have data confirming that those objects did change course. Your actions certainly saved lives. We don't presently know who did this, but hopefully, the data we received and you brought back will help us figure that out. It might not make much difference to the public either way because it's all over the media that the space station was destroyed. People are asking whether the crew and the MacMurchaids survived. Nothing is being said either way so far, and it will remain that way for the foreseeable future. Understood?"

Beltron and LaStarr simultaneously responded, "Yes, sir."

"With everything happening around the world and this incident," Tom continued, "we could be looking at war. Possibly even a worldwide war, which, as long as no nation goes nuclear, will be as close to a conventional war as is possible during this day and age. We'll know something soon since the joint chiefs and the president are currently meeting as to whether or not the United States will be involved. If the data shows that the space station was no accident, then we can expect a declaration of war. At least Robert and his family are safe for now."

After several days of analyzing the data and videos, the United States had confirmed that the space station was deliberately targeted for destruction. Before the United States officially declared war, those in Washington, DC held a memorial service for the MacMurchaids and crew members who supposedly died when the space station was destroyed. Only a select few knew the truth, but the memorial would build up national and possibly allied support for war. A few days later, the world was at war.

Chapter 14

Years of War

LIKE PREVIOUS MODERN WARS, the battles in this war were mainly fought on the ground, though bombing did also come into play. Then, those factions which did not have access to much started making their own bombs with different triggers to set them off when troops or vehicles tripped them. Drones came into heavy play as well to help take out encampments that were either hard to get to or heavily protected from troops.

As many had feared, radical groups started making what is known as dirty bombs. These were basically regular bombs, except that these ones had radioactive materials designed to scatter over a wide area when the bombs exploded. For a long time, the nuclear powers who were involved in the war withheld using their nuclear arsenals. But every government knew that if a radical group were to overthrow a nuclear-armed government, then the war could escalate and become catastrophic.

Unfortunately, as time passed, the radical groups that had started out foreign were joined by domestic radical groups, or "homegrown" radicals. This made it harder for governments to keep their troops abroad because they needed their troops to fight on the home front. This new world war did not seem to be easing up or slowing down. The United States government tried responding by ramping up technological advancements such as armored suits that would make troops more protected. These were the types of advancements that, like the nuclear bombs during World War II, might have helped bring the war to an end. However, there always seemed to be some sort of flaw or setback that prevented the United States from mass-producing these new implements of war.

As long as the various sides involved in the war could not see eye to eye, the war seemed as though it would linger on for a hundred years. And it almost did. Over ninety-eight years of war later, enough people had finally tired of war that alliances were formed and agreements were reached and the war finally ground to a halt. The human race finally wised up to the wrongs of the past and was again learning from them. It was finally time for worldwide healing of both humans and nature. Maybe there was true hope for the future after all. And the people of Earth, now at peace, could become explorers and discoverers again as they moved forward.

With the world now at peace, new transportation innovations and methods quickly improved, allowing people to more easily travel and help each other. After several more years had passed, the people of Earth began looking to space again as their possible future. The ancestors of the people on Earth had dreams of space exploration and discovery. And the people of Earth were ready to bring those dreams to fruition.

Chapter 15

The Awakening

"EXTERNAL COMMUNICATION SYSTEMS AND SENSORS INOPERATIVE. SECONDARY MALFUNCTIONING. ANALYSIS . . . FOREIGN SUBSTANCE COATING SYSTEMS." Odin pondered the problem for a few microseconds. "BEGIN REBIRTH OF SUBJECT ALPHA-ONE. REMOVE LOKI'S BREATH FROM VALHALLA AND SUBJECT'S CRADLE."

Two hours later, the Valhalla facility was entirely clear of Loki's Breath and was instead filled with an earth-like atmosphere. After another fifteen minutes, Robert MacMurchaid's sleep chamber opened, and he started to awaken. He slowly sat up and stretched. He then looked around and wondered where the technicians were. He slowly stood and tested his legs. After walking over to Odin's control panel, he pushed the Voice Response button. "Odin, please respond. Use voice synthesizer. Do you understand?"

"AFFIRMATIVE," Odin responded.

Robert pondered his question carefully to make sure to use

119

proper wording. "Explain: why are there no angels at rebirth?"

"ANGELS LEFT ONE WEEK, TWO DAYS, THREE HOURS, FORTY-FIVE MINUTES, AND FIFTEEN SEC-ONDS AFTER SUBJECTS' PSEUDO-DEATHS. FAILURE TO RETURN AT APPOINTED TIME."

Robert was extremely puzzled. He asked, "Possible reasons for angels' failure to return?"

"ONE WEEK, FOUR DAYS, ONE HOUR, SIXTEEN SECONDS AFTER SUBJECTS' DEATHS, ANGELS' HOME CEASED TO EXIST. EXPLANATION FROM MOTHER EARTH: GUIDED DEBRIS ITEMS ORBITING MOTHER EARTH TARGETED ANGELS' HOME. ANGELS HOME DESTROYED."

Robert realized Odin was referring to the space station and that there could only have been one response given to such an attack. "How long did the resulting war last?" he asked.

"NINETY-EIGHT YEARS, TEN MONTHS, TWO—"

"Stop, Odin!" Robert shouted. He already knew how long the war lasted from the information that was fed to him in his sleep chamber, but he was not willing to believe it until Odin confirmed it. Robert now realized how long he and his family had been in pseudo-death, and he staggered backward a bit. They had been in pseudo-death for 455 years. He already knew the reason Odin had finally woken him, but he asked Odin to confirm it anyway. "Odin, was my rebirth due to Lunar Sister passing through Comet NXZ-128's tail?"

"AFFIRMATIVE."

"Display Lunar Sister comet event on Alpha-One monitor."

"AFFIRMATIVE." Odin attempted to display the event,

but the display malfunctioned.

"Odin, display last Lunar Sister sensor reading," Robert instructed. He quickly scanned the display and discovered what the problem was. "Odin, give me an estimate of the depth of carbon-dioxide mixture flakes deposited on Lunar Sister's surface before sensors ceased functioning."

"ZERO-POINT-NINE-FIVE-SIX METERS."

Robert knew it would take more than himself to clear the carbon-dioxide mixture from the sensors. "Odin, begin rebirth of subjects Alpha-Two, Beta-One, Beta-Two, Beta-Three, and Beta-Four. Begin revitalization of Valhalla's garden. Restore life to Valhalla."

"AFFIRMATIVE." Almost immediately, lights came on in every room. Robotic workers took plants and seeds from storage and planted them in the terrain-lunar soil mixture. And the sleep chambers of Robert's family members were cleared of Loki's Breath. Less than two hours later, Robert heard the first questions from his family.

"Where is everybody?" Denise asked.

"Yeah, what's going on, Dad?" Tony chimed in.

"And when to we eat?" Troy asked before Robert could answer the other questions.

"I'll bring you up to date once we're seated in the dining area," Robert responded. He then escorted everyone to the dining area and asked them to be seated. "If you want something to eat or drink, go ahead and get it. This might take some time to get used to." Robert motioned toward the containers of supplies.

"Don't leave us in suspense, Dad," Kris pleaded.

"First," Robert began, "let me welcome you to the twenty-fifth century."

Almost in unison, the entire family belted out, "WHAT?!" Everyone had stopped what they were doing, and they were seemingly frozen in place.

"Is this a joke, Dad?" Nicole asked.

"It better be," Tony interjected. "My friends will be disappointed to death!" he said, laughing at his own joke, knowing that all of his friends had probably died centuries ago.

"No, this is not a joke, though I wish it were," Robert confirmed. "We've been in pseudo-death for about 455 years. You'll know it's true when you start tapping into your memories from what you were fed during pseudo-death." As the family did so, everyone quickly realized, to their dismay, that what Robert was saying was true.

"Why wake us now?" Troy asked. "Why not let us sleep forever?"

"The decision to wake you was mine," Robert replied. "There's a problem that Odin can't handle. It requires a human touch. If it's not handled, then over time, everything here will slowly and eventually go offline, including our sleep chambers. Odin, display on monitor Bravo-Zebra-Two last Lunar Sister sensor readings, estimate of carbon-dioxide mixture flake depth."

"AFFIRMATIVE."

"Carbon-dioxide mixture flake depth?" Denise asked with a puzzled look on her face.

"Yes, honey. We have snow on the moon in the form of some sort of dry-ice mixture. The moon passed through a comet's tail and was heavily dusted with the flaky mixture in the tail. The results are displayed on the monitor in front of you." Robert pointed to the screen. He let the family study the readout for a couple of minutes.

"SUBJECT ALPHA-ONE?"

"Yes, Odin?" Robert replied.

"SINCE ALL HUMAN SUBJECTS ARE REBORN, DIRECTIVES I MUST FOLLOW. ALL SUBJECTS VIEW MONITOR BRAVO-ZEBRA-ONE."

Everyone turned to the other monitor and watched what appeared there. The Universal Space Agency's emblem appeared on the screen, followed by Congressman Geoff Pitts. "Hello, my friends," he said. "Since you're viewing this, it means we were unable to wake you by our secondary date. Knowing your inquisitive nature, Robert, you have undoubtedly noticed the missing technicians and made inquiries of Odin. With that, plus the information fed to you while in pseudo-death, by now, you know that we went to war and why. In fact, at the time of this recording, we're *still* at war.

"We decided it was in your best interests if you were left in pseudo-death, especially since the space station was destroyed. We had to create a cover story that the test craft Valkyrie was also destroyed and that all crewmembers on the space station were killed. Many of us did not like this decision, but we wanted to keep everyone safe. People who knew of your continued existence were rotationally kept in secure locations throughout the war, and you were to be awakened once the war was over.

"After the space station's destruction, Odin was given directives to monitor all communication systems, especially our signals from Earth, and to continue feeding information to each of you. Odin was also instructed to continue feeding each of you information on subjects you're interested in and information you would need to run Valhalla in case we were unable to retrieve you once you were awakened. Odin has a nearly inexhaustible library of discs in a sub-cave near his core. He has also been recording ever since he first came online and was fully automated and self-reliant. His main directives during his lifespan have been to monitor you and record events on Earth. We calculated that he would be able to record somewhere in the range of 800 to 1,300 years of information, all of which would be accessible to you.

"Now on to other subjects," Geoff continued. "Most people on Earth believe that all of you are dead along with everyone from the space station. Since only a select few were privileged with the knowledge that you were, in fact, transferred to the moon, we felt that it was best for your safety during the war to let everyone else believe you had perished. Since even your own families were not privileged to the information about your mission, we had to let them believe the same—that you were dead.

"At a memorial service that was held for you, the military gave you each honorary officer ranks. The president signed a secret executive order making these ranks real and official if and when and you returned to earth. You were also each given honorary degrees from various universities for your efforts to promote education from space. I'm now going to pause for a moment and let the president address you. After he's through,

I'll continue and provide you with the information you'll need going forward."

With that, the screen changed from Geoff to the presidential seal and then to the president himself. "Hello, MacMurchaids. I wish I were speaking to you in person and that circumstances were different," the president began. "I've just signed an executive order stating that in the event you were for any reason left on the moon and were later awakened by Odin, the honorary ranks given to you at your memorial service would, in fact, become actual ranks. Since you're watching this message, I must presume that we were unable to send someone for you and that Odin has, for some reason, awakened you. Therefore, I now bestow your ranks upon you, as follows.

"Robert E. MacMurchaid: Major and Commander of Lunar Base Valhalla, including all equipment and facilities either lunar or terrain.

"Denise C. MacMurchaid: Captain and Second-in-Command.

"Kristophor M. MacMurchaid, Robert A. (Tony) MacMurchaid, Troy-Cook M. MacMurchaid, and Nicole R. MacMurchaid: you are all given the rank of lieutenant.

"Congratulations on these ranks. I wish the circumstances for giving them to you were different. Odin, Executive Order Echo-Tango-One-Point-Two-Five is effective immediately. Authorization is Zulu-Xray-Foxtrot-Three. Major MacMurchaid, I wish you and your family good luck, and may God watch over you all."

The presidential seal reappeared, and a few moments later, Geoff was back on the screen. "Some announcement, huh?" he said. "I agree with the president that I wish the circumstances were different. The executive order that he mentioned is stored digitally in Odin's memory bank and on discs, along with all the other information and data about you. And your personal belongings are stored in a sealed vault buried in a cavern deep under Cavanaugh Hill near Poteau, Oklahoma. All entrances to the cavern have been sealed. Odin can tell you more.

"Robert, since you're in command, you need to be a jack of all trades. I hope you can handle everything. And Denise, since you're second-in-command and are good with computers and languages, you're the communications officer. Kris, since you wanted to be a doctor, you're the medical officer. Tony, since you're good with your hands and are mechanically inclined, you're the engineering officer. Troy-Cook, since your interests involve martial arts and weapons, you're the security officer. And finally, Nicole, since your interests include plants and animals, you're the science officer. In executing your new roles, be sure to rely on the information and training you were fed during your pseudo-deaths.

"Oh, and speaking of animals, you might want Odin to awaken subjects Delta-On-Menagerie. We felt it would be interesting to see if domestic animals would be responsive to training while in pseudo-death. We only gave them simple instructions to learn—mainly obedience training but no attack training. And we didn't send just any animals; we sent your pets—your dog, Ears, your cat, Tabby, your ferret, Heidi, and all your other animals. We made sure you would have enough food to feed them—about a year or two years' worth. After that, you should be able to grow and manufacture your own food. Hopefully, you won't be there that long, though.

"There are other animals in pseudo-death at Valhalla as well," Geoff continued. They were placed there in case we decided to make Valhalla a permanent base. They were chosen for usefulness, practicability, and enjoyment. You'll find a list of animals along with corresponding codes on disc number One-One-Three-Five-Echo. You can awaken them as you see fit.

"Well, that's about all the information I have for you at this point in time, but I hope I'll be able to send more messages at a later time. Good luck to each of you and all of you. You might have become Earth's future in more than the way we originally intended." The monitor went blank.

"Well, let's not celebrate our new ranks right now," Robert suggested. "We have too much work to do to keep this facility functional and try to communicate with Earth again." The entire family silently and sullenly nodded their agreement.

Chapter 16

Working on a Solution

THE MACMURCHAID FAMILY looked back toward monitor Bravo-Zebra-Two to see the chemical makeup of the carbon-dioxide mixture that had blanketed the moon. They wanted to see if they could do something to quickly remove the mixture from the sensors on the lunar surface. "There doesn't seem to be any volatile chemicals, though there are some unknown elements listed here," Robert observed. "Since carbon dioxide goes from solid to gas when heat is applied, that might be the solution for clearing the equipment," he suggested.

"Geoff said we were given the knowledge to run and take care of Valhalla," Robert continued. "So, we should already know of items we can use or assemble to project heat on the mixture. Everyone spread out and search for those items. We'll all meet in the Valkyrie hangar when we're done searching. The door to that hangar seems to be the one with the least mixture in contact with it, so it should be the easiest door to clear. This stuff might not be that thick, but the last temperature readings say that it's extremely cold, so the other doors might be frozen in place. Okay, let's get moving."

In response to Robert's instructions, the other family members got busy. In the back of their minds, they all knew it would be bad to wake up after so many years only to slowly die due to equipment shutting down. Even if someone knew about the family and came for them, those people wouldn't be able to get in under the current conditions. All doors to the Valhalla facility were likely frozen shut.

After the family gathered many items, they met in Valkyrie's hangar. Robert surveyed the items and said, "Okay, these should work for what we need. Unfortunately, the valves outside are frozen in the off position, and I don't want anyone to touch them until we clean them in case that mixture can freeze *us* as well. We'll have to connect to the valves between the inner door and outer door. Let's get these things assembled so we can get started." Robert was speaking with great urgency, which made the other family members somewhat nervous.

Once the family had assembled a heating torch, Robert spoke again. "This should work fine. I'll take Tony with me to do the job since he's the stronger of the two older boys. The rest of you need to monitor our progress and keep me informed of how things are improving or worsening. Tony, let's go get into our spacesuits. We have some tough work ahead of us."

After Robert and Tony had gotten their gear on and ensured that it was all sealed up, they headed to the inner hangar door. "Odin, open inner Valkyrie hangar door," Robert instructed. Within seconds, they heard pistons moving, and then the door opened. Robert and Tony moved the equipment and themselves into the area between the inner hangar door and outer hangar door. Once they were inside, Robert said, "Odin, close inner door." Slowly, the inner door closed, and Denise verified for Robert that the pins had locked the door in place.

Robert and Tony hooked up two hoses to the backup valves between the doors. "Everything looks good here," Robert observed. "Luckily, they learned from early liquid propulsion rockets and missiles that new synthetic material keeps the propellants from eating through their containers. Otherwise, we would have been in a world of hurt before we were awakened!"

"You're right about that, Dad," Tony agreed.

"Okay, Denise," Robert continued. "Let's go over this before we open the outer door. We start with exceptionally low psi on both propellants. I do not want our makeshift torch to become a rocket! That would be bad for Tony and me."

"Roger that, honey," Denise confirmed. "You both be careful out there. I want you both to come back."

"Don't worry, Mom; we'll be careful," Tony assured her. "We both want to get back inside with you guys."

"Okay, Odin, open outer door," Robert instructed. "The pistons began to move. Once the pistons were clear, the door began to open. Then, suddenly, the door stopped and appeared jammed in place. "Odin, what has happened?" Robert asked with concern in his voice.

"CARBON-DIOXIDE MIXTURE HAS BLOCKED DOOR FROM FULLY OPEN," Odin informed them.

"Well, folks, the door is stuck," Robert said with a somewhat calmer tone. "But I think it's at least open enough for us to get through. We'll begin using the torch where the door is open and work our way around it. Remember to start at exceptionally low psi until I say to increase it by one psi per increase, Denise. Hopefully, with luck, we'll not need much flow pressure to clear things. Okay, begin flow, honey." Within a short time, the two propellants mixed within the torch and began shooting out flames. "Okay, hold it there for now until we're both outside."

Since there were not many carbon-dioxide mixture flakes where Robert first aimed the torch, they cleared away rather quickly. The heat was enough to change the flake mixture into a gaseous form, but the gas did not dissipate as Robert had hoped and expected. Regardless, Robert and Tony were able to clear enough of the flakes for them to get the outer hangar door open far enough for them to squeeze themselves through it and reach the outside.

"Honey, keep me informed of sensor readings," Robert instructed Denise.

"I will. You two, please be careful," Denise responded.

As Robert and Tony began using the torch to clear more of the door, they realized that they needed an increase in the flow pressure of the propellants. "First increase of psi needed," Robert said to Denise. Then, after a few seconds, he said, "Second increase needed." Now, the torch seemed to be doing a better job clearing around the door and the surrounding area. "That's good for now," Robert said.

Once Robert and Tony had fully cleared the door area, Odin finished opening the door. Tony verified by stating, "Outer door fully open." Once they knew it was completely open, they moved further away from the door and toward some of the Valhalla facility's outdoor sensors and equipment, clearing a wide pathway as they went along. Then, as Tony looked around, he noticed something and alerted his dad. "Hey, Dad, stop for a minute. Am I imagining things, or is that mixture dissipating even though we haven't hit it with the heat yet?"

Robert stopped moving forward and turned to look where Tony was pointing. "I don't think you're imagining things because if you are, then so am I. I see it, too."

Denise cut in, saying, "What are you two seeing out there? The outer cameras still aren't working."

"Mom, it appears that what we heated has made a cloud, and the cloud is affecting the flakey mixture near it. It's as though the mixture is helping to clear itself via the cloud due to a physical reaction or a chemical reaction. Once the sensors are back online, we'll have to study this closely," Tony suggested.

"Please be careful. And keep me informed if this continues," Denise said.

"Roger that, Mom."

Robert went back to clearing the area. But instead of going about it as he had earlier—by keeping the heat on certain spots until the mixture was completely gone—he tried holding the heat there only long enough for the mixture to change to the gaseous form. The father and son's suspicions from their observations were confirmed. Once the flaky mixture changed to the gaseous form, the gas continued to clear the mixture on its own even though the heat source had been removed. Robert relayed this information to Denise, and she made a note of it.

"Okay, we can speed this up now and cover more area with less fuel," Robert said. "This isn't as bad as we first thought. But I'm worried about what that mixture will do next. Let's get this done and get back inside as soon as possible, Tony. By the way, have you noticed that we're not moving like we did when we first arrived at Valhalla? I don't mean the suits making a difference; it's something else. I vaguely noticed it before, after I ordered Odin to wake everyone."

"I hadn't paid attention to it until you just mentioned it, Dad. But yes, moving around does feel different," Tony agreed.

When Robert and Tony stopped for a moment to see what they had cleared so far, they noticed that the area cleared was bigger than where they had used the torch. "Let's go back in and monitor this strange event happening out here," Robert suggested to Tony. "Mom has the flow of propellants cut off for now. Let's return to the outer door."

"Okay, Dad. But is there something wrong?"

"We'll talk when we're back inside, Tony. Denise, if enough sensors are clear, then have Odin monitor this area and the areas surrounding it. We're coming in now." Once Robert and Tony had the torch and its hoses back between the two hangar doors, Robert said, "Odin, close outer door." The door shut and sealed, and Robert then said, "Odin, open inner door." Once the inner door was open, they took all the equipment into the hanger, and Robert said, "Odin, close inner door." Once the door was closed and sealed, everyone helped move the equipment to a safe place while Robert and Tony got out of their spacesuits.

"Okay, Robert, now explain why you stopped clearing that flaky mixture," Denise demanded of her husband.

"Let's go back to the dining area so you can listen to me speak with Odin about it, and maybe you'll get your explanation." Everyone in the family headed to the dining area and sat down.

"Odin? Tony and I noticed a couple of interesting things while we were outside and before we went out there to work. Do you have any data from the sensors that we cleared?"

"YES, MAJOR MACMURCHAID."

"Have you begun to analyze what was happening in the area that was cleared?"

"ANALYSIS NOT COMPLETE BUT ONGOING."

"Any speculation as to what was happening in the cleared area?"

"BEGINNING ANALYSIS SHOWS POSSIBLE CHEMICAL INTERACTION BETWEEN CARBON-DIOXIDE MIXTURE AND PROPELLENTS."

"Odin, continue analysis."

"AFFIRMATIVE."

Turning to his family, Robert began to explain why he had cut short the task of clearing the mixture outside their facility. "While we were working out there, Tony pointed out a strange reaction happening with the mixture. We both noticed it. So, now I'm going to ask all of you if you've noticed any changes since we were awakened. Have you?"

"What do you mean, Daddy?" Nicole asked.

"Have any of you noticed that our movements have changed slightly compared to when we first arrived at Valhalla?" Robert asked, clarifying his original question.

The family members all began to think about Robert's question. And then, they all answered some version of, "Maybe, a little."

"I'm not certain," Robert responded, "but I think the gravity might have changed slightly since we first arrived here because we aren't moving with that slight bounce we used to have. I'm wondering if the comet might have increased the moon's rotation slightly. I'll have Odin check on that once all the sensors are cleared. For now, let's just relax and wait for Odin's analysis of what's happening in the area we cleared. Does anyone want a snack or a drink while we wait?"

Chapter 17

The Solution's Surprise

A FTER ROBERT WAITED for what seemed to him like an eternity, Odin finally spoke. "MAJOR MACMUR-CHAID, INITIAL ANALYSIS COMPLETE. BUT CONTINUED ANALYSIS ONGOING."

"Odin, give initial analysis," Robert instructed.

"CLOUD IS LINGERING IN THE AREA SINCE GRAVITY IS NO LONGER 0.1667 OF EARTH MOTHER GRAVITY. GRAVITY HAS INCREASED TO 0.32833 OF EARTH MOTHER GRAVITY."

"Is there a possibility that this increase is related to Comet NXZ-128 passing close to Lunar Sister?"

"ANALYSIS DOES NOT HAVE ENOUGH DATA DUE TO SOME SENSORS STILL NOT FUNCTIONING AND COMMUNICATIONS WITH EARTH MOTHER NOT BEING REESTABLISHED."

"Understood. Is the size of the area cleared increasing?"

"YES. BUT INCREASE HAS SLOWED."

"Does analysis indicate whether the increase was a thermal

or chemical reaction?"

"ANALYSIS INDICATES THERMAL REACTION BE-GINS THE INCREASE BUT INCREASE CONTINUES BECAUSE OF CHEMICAL REACTION CREATING A BEGINNING ATMOSPHERE."

"Understood," Robert responded to Odin as everyone else looked on with perplexed expressions.

"What?! What does *that* mean?" Nicole asked her father.

Robert tried to calm them all down and began to explain his thoughts as to why there was an atmosphere beginning to form near the Valkyrie hangar door. "I don't know exactly what propellants we're using here. But thanks to my time working on the Titan II Intercontinental Ballistic Missile, I have a basic idea of why this is happening. The chemicals in the propellants mix together, creating heat and water, and they release other mixtures of chemicals as they burn. This carbon-dioxide mixture that the comet left has quite a list of minute amounts of other chemicals, including ones that we cannot identify."

Robert paused, thought for a moment, then continued. "The chemicals from both inputs—the propellants and the carbon-dioxide mixture—are mixing and dividing into the type of elements we would expect to see in an atmosphere like the one close to Earth. The unidentified chemicals in the mixture from the comet might be helping to create the atmosphere that is forming close to the lunar surface. Then, when you add in the increase in lunar gravity, you have an explanation as to why this new atmosphere is not escaping out into space. This is just my rough guess for now as to what's happening. We won't know for sure until we get more sensors cleared and Odin can do a better analysis."

Robert could see that although his family generally understood what he was saying, they were still puzzled by the events happening outside. "Odin, based on our present data and analysis, would flying the lunar shuttle close to Lunar Sister's surface produce the same type of clearing effect as the torch?" Robert asked.

"USING PRIMARY ANALYSIS, IT IS POSSIBLE IT COULD WORK. BUT FURTHER ANALYSIS NEEDED TO INCREASE PERCENTAGE OF CERTAINTY."

"Understood, Odin. We'll try that option to see if we can clear the mixture from the outdoor sensors faster," Robert announced to his family. "With more sensors coming back online, Odin might be able to speculate whether the new atmosphere will do us good or bad. Maneuvering the lunar shuttle close to the lunar surface will be tricky because we'll have to clear the crater, its rim, and the surrounding area. And we'll have to keep the shuttle around eight to ten feet above the surface and objects in order to send enough heat down to help start the chemical reaction that is needed to clear the mixture. Hopefully, we aren't making a mistake by doing this. But we have no choice other than to try it if we want to survive. Odin, are the sensors near lunar shuttle bay door working?" Robert asked.

"AFFIRMATIVE. SURFACE MATERIAL OF LUNAR SISTER APPEARS TO HAVE SHIELDED THEM FROM CARBON-DIOXIDE MIXTURE FLAKES."

"Odin, does the outer door for the lunar shuttle bay function properly?"

"ACTUATING DOOR TO CONFIRM." Time seemed to pass slowly while waiting to see if the door would fully open and close. But Odin eventually said, "AFFIRMATIVE. DOOR FUNCTIONING NORMAL."

"Thank you, Odin. Please communicate with lunar shuttle to check if it's functional and ready to proceed with flight plan."

"AFFIRMATIVE."

"Okay, everyone, we'll do this, but I'll be the only one flying the shuttle, with Odin as backup." Robert raised his hand to stop everyone from responding to what he had said. "With Odin communicating with the shuttle, there's less chance of anything bad happening. But just in case, if something goes wrong with shuttle, I want Kris and Tony ready as a rescue team. Or, if something happens to me and the shuttle is still functional, then Odin can fly it back to the bay."

Robert could see that Denise was about to protest, so he put his hand up again to stop her. "There is no debate on this, Denise. I received more training input while in pseudo-death than any of you, so I can react to many situations related to the shuttle. Plus, I think there was a positive side effect from being in pseudo-death for so long. Having sensors that fed our brains information has improved the part of the brain that deals with ESP, telepathy, etcetera. I don't know if you've noticed something strange that I have, but I at times seem to hear Odin before his voice comes through the audio speakers. If this develops more in all of us, maybe we can use it to react quicker."

Robert left and changed into his spacesuit. He then boarded

the shuttle. Once in the shuttle, he said, "Odin, open inner shuttle bay door to allow shuttle into launch position."

"AFFIRMATIVE."

Once the door was fully open, the shuttle was maneuvered into launch position. Robert then instructed, "Odin, close inner shuttle bay door."

"AFFIRMATIVE."

Once the inner door was closed, Robert's next instruction was, "Odin, open outer shuttle bay door."

"AFFIRMATIVE."

Once the outer door was open, the shuttle's engines started up. "Odin, once the shuttle is outside, close outer shuttle bay door. Then, assist with the shuttle controls to ensure flight level over every object is within the range set and the speed you calculated."

"AFFIRMATIVE."

Robert headed, in the shuttle, to the start coordinates for his flyover to remove the carbon-dioxide mixture. With Odin's assistance, Robert flew the pattern they had planned to be most effective at clearing everything they needed to free themselves of the frozen mixture. After what seemed like an eternity for his family back at Valhalla, Robert finally finished the pattern and began to head back to the shuttle bay. "Odin, open outer shuttle bay door."

"AFFIRMATIVE."

Once the door was fully open, the shuttle flew in and landed. "Odin, close outer shuttle bay door."

"AFFIRMATIVE."

Once the outer door was closed and sealed, Robert continued, saying, "Odin, open inner shuttle bay door."

"AFFIRMATIVE."

Once the inner door was fully open, the shuttle was maneuvered back into the bay and into its designated space. "Odin, close inner shuttle bay door."

"AFFIRMATIVE."

After the inner bay door was shut, Robert got out of the shuttle. "Odin, are all sensors and equipment in the area we cleared on Lunar Sister operational?" he asked.

"AFFIRMATIVE. THEY ARE REACHING OPERATIONAL SPECIFICATIONS. DATA IS BEING RECEIVED."

"Thank you, Odin. Once you complete your computations of the new data combined with the old data, alert me."

"AFFIRMATIVE. YOU ARE WELCOME."

Robert took particular note of Odin's last words and contemplated whether Odin was programmed with such a response or it was possible that the growing connection he felt with Odin had produced the proper response. But that wasn't important right then. So, Robert changed out of his spacesuit and returned to his family members, who were eagerly awaiting him. They were glad he was back and safe.

Denise directed her husband to look at the data on the monitor. Robert responded to what he was seeing by asking, "What in the Sam Hill is going on here? According to these readings, there is a proto-atmosphere similar to early Earth forming outside. We'll have to wait for Odin to receive enough data to complete his computations and maybe give us a better idea as to why this happened. Odin, are the satellite uplinks reestablished?"

"AFFIRMATIVE. THOUGH A NUMBER OF SATEL-

LITES ARE OPERATING AT MINIMAL CAPACITY, THEY'RE RECEIVING DATA TO HELP THEM RETURN TO FULL CAPACITY."

"Odin, are we able to receive visuals of Earth Mother and Lunar Sister?"

"AFFIRMATIVE."

"Please display visuals of each." On the large monitor in the room, side-by-side images of Earth and the moon appeared. "Though Earth appears different than it used to, most likely due to the long war," Robert noted, "it looks as though its atmosphere is basically the same. But the image of the moon from the side facing the sun appears fuzzy. Odin, is the image of Lunar Sister distorted due to a failure within the satellite?"

"NEGATIVE."

"Is the image showing a similar event as what is occurring outside here at Valhalla, on the dark side of the moon?"

"INSUFFICIENT DATA AT THIS TIME. BUT PROBABILITY HIGH THAT SIDE OF LUNAR SISTER FACING SOLAR FATHER HAS AFFECTED CARBON-DIOXIDE MIXTURE SIMILARLY FROM SOLAR FATHER'S HEAT AND SOLAR RADIATION. MORE DATA NEEDED."

"Understood, Odin. Are you monitoring Earth Mother communications?"

"AFFIRMATIVE."

"Do they have any mention of Earth Mother being affected by the comet?"

"AFFIRMATIVE. LITTLE EFFECT ON EARTH MOTHER EXCEPT POSSIBLE DECREASE IN SIZE OF HOLE IN OZONE. EARTH MOTHER COMMUNICATIONS IN-

DICATE UNKNOWN FOG FORMING ON LUNAR SISTER THAT COMPUTES AS A POSSIBLE ATMOSPHERE FORMING."

"Odin, continue monitoring and continue your computations. Thank you."

"AFFIRMATIVE. YOU ARE WELCOME."

This time, everyone noticed Odin's response to Robert. "What was that 'you are welcome' all about?" Denise asked Robert.

"There are two possibilities. First, Odin might have been programmed to respond that way. Or second, the link that I suspect developed between Odin and us while we were in pseudo-death for so long has given him the ability to respond the same way we would. I'll ask him about it later. But for now, we need to figure out what's going on with the atmosphere that's forming here at Valhalla, on the dark side of the moon, and the one that seems to be forming on the side of the moon that's facing the sun. We have most of the data from our dark side of the moon, which is the data Odin is using for his computations. But we can only speculate as to what is happening to create an atmosphere on the other side of the moon."

Robert paused and thought for a moment, then continued. "The reason I want Odin to monitor Earth's communications is to see what answers they might provide. I suspect that the reason Earth was not affected by the comet in the same way the moon was is that, like most comet debris, this comet's debris burned up while entering Earth's atmosphere. That might explain the hole in the ozone shrinking. Hopefully, the effects here will be positive, too."

"I'll agree to wait for more data concerning this proto-atmosphere," Denise said. "But I notice more wrong with Earth than just signs of war. Look!" Denise had the whole family look at the image of Earth on the monitor again. "Some of the land masses on Earth have changed. They appear upside down! What could have caused *that*?" she asked.

"Well, Mom," Tony piped up, "the magnetic field could have shifted, causing Earth's crust to shift too."

"Another possibility," Troy added, "is that the war was so bad that it caused earthquakes and caused volcanoes to erupt, causing the land masses to look different."

"Why not *both* possibilities?" Nicole suggested.

"It could have been those things," Kris added. "Or there might have been multiple impacts. Or maybe the magnetic field of the comet could have added to the effects of *any* of these possibilities."

"These are definitely still our children," Robert said to Denise with a chuckle. "I think they would have come up with these possibilities even before they were given 455 years of education. Sooner or later, I'm sure we'll tap into the information we were fed during pseudo-death that will explain why the Earth looks the way it does now."

"This seems like something out of one of the science fiction movies we used to watch before our mission," Denise pointed out. She was visibly upset by Earth's new appearance. "I wonder if people on Earth knew these changes were happening."

"They might have *suspected* something was happening, but in reality, they could probably only see what was happening close to where they were on earth," Robert supposed. "It depends on what all was destroyed on Earth. If the systems that monitor these kinds of changes were not destroyed, then anyone with access to them likely would have seen the changes occurring, though they would not have been able to share their observations with too many people. It certainly *is* similar to the movies we used to watch, except in this case, Earth hasn't righted itself yet." Robert felt bad that Denise was so concerned and knew his words didn't help.

"Think of what's happened since the end of the war and the beginning of peace," Robert continued. "The people of Earth have grown together and progressed as one family. They've worked to rebuild things and to help nature. They've been able to accomplish a lot by learning from their mistakes of the past, and they're now working toward a future that benefits everyone on Earth. Perhaps someday, we'll even meet the descendants of those we left behind and see how they're now living. We already miss those who went before us, but we're still alive through their descendants, and we can possibly work together as a family to make a better future for our further descendants." When Robert finished, he pulled Denise close to him and held her tightly.

"When you put it that way, we do have something to look forward to," Denise said, feeling somewhat reassured. "For now, we need to get past this moment in time, and hopefully, everything will turn out for the better." Denise turned toward Robert, and they kissed.

"Get a room!" Tony said jokingly. His parent scowled at him, but they were glad that after 455 years, their children had not lost their sense of humor. Tony put his hands over his face as though he were protecting himself from the view of the kiss. "Okay, okay, I apologize," he said. "By the way, Niki noticed something on another monitor that she wants you both to see." They all headed over to the monitor Nicole was looking at.

"What's up, darling?" Denise asked her daughter.

"Look at the monitor. These images are from newer satellites and not the older ones," Nicole informed her parents. The images are much clearer and have greater definition to them than anything I've ever seen, but it's what they're seeing that really amazes me. One of the images shows a high-earth-orbit station with plants and trees growing under a clear dome on a portion of the station."

While looking at the monitor, Robert noticed that another image displayed there peered through the depths of what the family would have known as the Indian Ocean back when they were still on Earth. Now, there appeared to be a multi-domed city on the sea floor, under the ocean. "Those are amazing images," he said. "And they seem to prove what I was just saying: that the people of Earth have done much better since worldwide peace began than they did when we used to live there. Keep it up, Niki; you're doing a great job monitoring things for us," Robert encouraged his daughter. "Let us know if you receive any more images of interest from the satellites."

Denise turned to Robert and asked, "You realize those images indicate that we might not be up here alone, don't you?"

"I do," Robert confirmed. "I won't get my hopes up, but once we get past this proto-atmosphere puzzle, I want to check into the possibility of contacting others. Sound good?"

Denise nodded. She wondered if there might even be others on the moon with them. But her thoughts were interrupted by Odin alerting the family.

"SENSORS FULLY OPERATIONAL. SATELLITE UP-LINKS ARE NOMINAL. PROTO-ATMOSPHERE IS SLOW-LY ENVELOPING LUNAR SISTER FROM BOTH SIDES. ATMOSPHERE IS BECOMING MORE LIKE EARTH MOTHER'S ATMOSPHERE." Odin halted for a moment, then said, "ALERT! CRAFT APPROACHING VALHALLA VICINITY."

The MacMurchaids became extremely excited but also nervous in response to the alert. Robert asked, "Odin, is it robotic? Or does the craft have any lifeforms on board?"

"ONE LIFEFORM ON CRAFT. FEMALE. CRAFT TRA-JECTORY NOW CHANGING. NOW ON DIRECT COURSE FOR CRATER JULES VERNE AND VALHALLA."

"Understood, Odin," Robert confirmed. "Approximate time to crater?"

"16.37 MINUTES AT CURRENT VELOCITY."

"Understood, Odin," Robert said again before turning to Denise. "Well, honey, I guess we'll have to greet our first guest." Denise looked nervous but nodded, knowing they had no choice in the matter.

"Odin," Robert continued, "when the craft is closer, send a message to the lifeform that the MacMurchaid family of six will greet her at the shuttle bay. Provide lighting to show her the entrance."

"AFFIRMATIVE."

With that, the family readied themselves as best they could for their first-ever visitor at Valhalla.

Chapter 18

Human Contact

ODIN FOLLOWED THE directives Robert gave him and sent a message to the occupant of the visiting craft before it reached Valhalla. After sending the message, he lit the area around the shuttle bay entrance and opened the outer door. The craft slowed its approach, as if the woman inside was hesitant about what to do next. Eventually, the craft landed inside the outer door. Odin then shut and sealed the outer door and opened the inner door, allowing the craft to maneuver into its final landing spot. Once the craft was safely inside Valhalla, Odin shut and sealed the inner door, and the craft's propulsion system shut down.

The MacMurchaids had nervously gathered across the bay from the craft, not sure what to expect from their visitor. They assumed that if there was any threat, Odin would have already detected it and warned them. Even before she exited the craft, the family could see the look of disbelief on the woman's face. It took her a few moments to gather her composure before she finally exited the craft.

Robert greeted the woman—the first guest they had had anywhere in over 455 years—by saying, "Welcome to Valhalla, the home of the MacMurchaid family." As he spoke, Robert gestured toward his family, indicating that they were the Mac-Murchaids.

The woman was still slightly shocked but was able to ask, "Are you *really* the MacMurchaids? You were reported dead back in the first half of the twenty-first century. How is it possible that you're still alive and still here? I have so many questions."

Denise took the lead and responded, "We fully expected a lot of questions. But please don't worry; we are, in fact, the MacMurchaids. Luckily, the rumors of our deaths were false. We can explain things to you in a while, but first, let's introduce oursel—"

The woman cut Denise off by saying, "There is no need for introductions because I already know you from my ancestry. I'm a descendant of your brother-in-law, Denise. My name is Frances Murchison. My lineage is through his daughter, Layna. I've seen photos of you and your family many times, and I know each of your names and a little bit about you already. I've also watched all the recordings that have been passed down from the twenty-first century. You're the most famous family members out of all our ancestors. I'm just shocked that you're still alive and that you still appear as you did when the space station was destroyed. I have so many questions that I want to ask! But first, I have to be sure that I'm not dreaming."

The MacMurchaids could see Frances's excitement. Robert hoped they might be able to calm her down by taking her to the dining area where everyone could sit down. "You're definitely not dreaming," he told her. "Let's go this way, to the dining area, and we'll do our best to explain things to you there."

Denise showed Frances the way as the rest of the family followed. "This is our dining area," Denise informed her. "It isn't much, but we hope to make it more pleasant in the future." As she spoke, she smiled toward Robert.

Once everyone was seated, Robert began to explain things to Frances. "What people from our time didn't know is that we, the MacMurchaids, had a larger mission than just visiting the space station. But only a select few people other than us knew about it. We were flown here to this station—known as Valhalla—for an experiment that was conducted with the hope of opening space travel and exploration to other families. We were all put into a state of hibernation, which was only scheduled to last three months. But apparently, after we were put into that state, war broke out on Earth, the space station was destroyed, and no one returned to get us."

Robert paused and took a sip of water before continuing. "While in hibernation, we were still receiving information, which was fed directly to our brains. So, we know most of the history from then until now and much more. We were only awakened by Odin—the computer charged with the safety of this facility and all who are in it—due to the mess caused by the comet. The station's sensors were going offline, and other equipment was affected. This facility would have died a slow death had Odin not woken us. Once we were awake, we began to try and solve the problems before us. The atmospheric phenomenon you might have noticed outside this facility is the result of our attempts at a solution to the problem. This is, of course, just a brief and oversimplified version of our story. But what is your story, Frances? What is it that has brought you here?"

Frances responded, "I was sent here to investigate the changes that are happening in this area. I wasn't sure what I would find. But I definitely did not expect to find all of you here. We didn't know that there was anything like this facility on the dark side of the moon. We figured we'd maybe find a few old space relics from the twentieth and twenty-first centuries but definitely not you or your facility. We recently picked up a signal that something was happening here that was similar to what we've been seeing on the lit side of the moon. And we thought it would take longer than this for solar radiation to cause the same effect here, on the dark side of the moon, that we've been seeing. So, I was sent here to investigate the cause. My sensors did not pick up your facility because they were set to detect the anomaly instead. It wasn't until the lights came on here that I noticed your facility."

"Well, we did think about keeping our facility hidden, in case you were a threat," Robert informed Frances. "But with it clear that you were getting closer and not going away, we figured we might as well roll the dice and roll out the welcome mat. As far as the event on the lit side of the moon, as you call it, we briefly pondered its cause. We believe it was caused by an interaction between solar radiation and the mixture the comet deposited. We also checked for possible effects of Earth going through the comet's tail. And we found that the hole in Earth's ozone is shrinking. We figured there might have been minor tremors and odd tidal events on Earth as the comet passed near. But we're shocked at how drastically different Earth looks now compared to when we left it."

"I'm sure by now your superiors are wondering why you haven't reported in yet, Frances," Denise posited.

"They might be. But they already know I've landed at a facility that we didn't know about. They'll definitely be surprised when I report in and tell them what's here. However, there seems to be some interference in here that's preventing me from doing so."

Robert nodded to Troy, and Troy spoke to Odin, saying, "Security clearance T-C-One-Alpha. Allow outside communications for our guest."

"AFFIRMATIVE," Odin responded. And he immediately cleared the interference.

Frances was noticeably amazed by what she was witnessing. A voice came across the comm that was attached to her shirt: "Lieutenant Murchison, please respond."

Frances quickly responded. "I'm here and okay. Conditions here are similar to what we're experiencing on the lit side. But the reasons are different. I'll give you a full explanation when I return to base. Out!" She paused for a moment, then said, "I'm not sure how I'm going to explain your existence to them."

"Maybe we could help with that if we were there in person," Denise suggested. She then jokingly said, "You could do as our children did in times of old and simply say, 'Mom, we've invited some guests to dinner' without prior warning." Denise and Robert chuckled, but the kids shook their heads in embarrassment.

Frances grinned and said, "I'm not sure my father would understand that or accept it. But maybe something similar might work."

The family gave Frances a brief tour of the Valhalla facility. They then provided her with a little more information, including that a garden had recently been planted there and that there were animals still in hibernation. Frances found all of this fascinating.

"Do you think we'd all fit into your craft, or shall we take ours?" Denise asked Frances.

"Everyone will fit," Frances answered. "Besides, you'll need the code to enter our facility, and I can't just give it to you. So, you'll need to come with me."

"Yes, and I'm sure it will be easier for you to explain things to everyone on the lit side if we arrive with you," Robert pointed out. "That way, we can fill in all the blanks."

"I would have to agree with you there," Frances said. "But are you sure about leaving this facility unattended?"

"As we mentioned earlier, Odin has full control of this facility as well as all of its defensive mechanisms," Robert stated. "And although I'm not completely sure, I'm quite certain that my family and I have a special way to communicate with Odin while we're away." Robert winked at his family, and they all grinned back at him.

Everyone loaded into Frances's craft and got seated and buckled in. She was amazed to see the inner door to Valhalla open for them without anyone saying a word. She maneuvered her craft through the inner door and then waited for the door to close. Once that door closed and the outer door opened,

Frances steered her craft across the moonscape and back to her facility. Though she remained curious about the doors opening on their own, she figured the MacMurchaids would include that in their explanation to her and her father once they arrived at their destination.

The MacMurchaids stayed fairly quiet on the flight as they admired the moonscape they were passing over. Finally, they neared the facility that Frances called home.

Chapter 19

Back to Civilization, Lunar Style

AS FRANCES'S CRAFT approached her facility, she got on the comm and said, "Security clearance: Frances-One-One-Alpha-Zulu. Clear bay of all personnel. Order number One-Alpha-One-Zulu."

A man's voice responded over the comm, saying, "Understood. Clearance to land. Order will be followed."

As the craft slowed, the MacMurchaids noticed a system of doors on the ground that slid open. Once the doors were open, Frances controlled her craft's descent through them. The doors closed behind the craft, and Frances told her passengers, "We'll have to wait for the bay to refill with air," which they did. As the door on the craft began to open, the MacMurchaids could see a gentleman approaching. Frances says, "Let me exit first, okay? I don't want to frighten him."

As the gentleman got closer, he asked Frances, "Why the unusual orders?"

She responded, "Father, I would like to introduce you to our long-lost relatives, the MacMurchaids."

"What?!" her father responded, with a perplexed look on his face.

Frances waved for the family to exit the craft. "While I was investigating the oddity on the other side of the moon, I met up with the MacMurchaids!"

Her father, still shocked, said again, "What?!"

Robert spoke. "It's all right, sir. We'd be happy to explain things to my brother's descendants."

Colonel Thomas Murchison was still somewhat shocked at seeing these people alive. But, like his daughter, he recognized them from photos and knew that they really were the MacMurchaids. "I'm sorry for my reaction," he said. "My name is Thomas Murchison. And you're all more than welcome here. It's just a shock to see people everyone thought had died hundreds of years ago." Everyone grinned as Thomas and Frances escorted the MacMurchaids to more comfortable surroundings.

Once everyone was seated, Robert said, "I know you'll have plenty of questions you want to ask, and once others find out we're alive, they will, too. But first, let me tell you some of our story. My family's flight into space was not limited to the space station. Instead, we were sent on a bigger mission: to help further space exploration and discovery. The name 'Valhalla' that was mentioned prior to our mission was not a reference to our mission itself, but instead to the facility your daughter discovered us at today. My entire family was part of an experiment that would be used to help future space exploration. We left the space station days before its destruction and were put into a form of suspended animation known to us as pseudo-death."

Robert paused for a moment, letting Thomas and Frances soak in his statements. He then continued. "Pseudo-death was induced by a special gas known as Loki's Breath, which slows bodily functions down so much that a doctor would think a person under the gas was dead. However, our bodies were still alive, and we could even continue to learn in that state. After we were under the gas, our technicians and flight crew left Valhalla and, as we learned from information we were fed during sleep, made it safely back to the space station and then to Earth after the space station was destroyed. With the space station gone, nobody could return to wake us.

"Our facility's control computer, Odin, kept monitoring us and kept control of all of Valhalla. As war continued raging on Earth, we continued to survive in a state of hibernation. And we continued to receive information for years and centuries until a critical situation caused Odin to wake us. Specifically, Valhalla would have slowly died if sensors and equipment on its surface were not cleared of deposits left by the comet, which was a task only humans could complete. So, after 455 years, my family and I were awakened and brought up to speed, and we began clearing the sensors and equipment. There are many other details, but that's the gist of what has brought us here today," Robert finished.

Thomas was impressed with the story. "My main question for now is, how were you able to change the mess the comet left from solid to gas?" he asked. "On our lit side of the moon, we're hit with solar radiation that helps clear things. But on your dark side of the moon, that's not possible until the moon's rotation faces you to the sun."

Robert responded, "We still have a craft that was used to bring technicians to our facility on Lunar Sister, which is what we call the moon. And we used the craft's liquid thruster propellants to help clear the mess. Prior to doing so, we were also able to build and use a flamethrower to free one of Valhalla's doors and clear a few sensors. When we saw how well that worked, we switched to using the spacecraft. It required precision flying and maneuvering, but with Odin's help managing the altitude and speed, we were able to pull it off and cover the entire area we needed to clear in a relatively short time."

"Another question I have is, why did you so promptly reveal yourselves to Frances?" Thomas asked.

Robert responded again. "My first instinct was to do what many military members would have done and keep my family and myself hidden. I also thought about blocking all communications from our facility. And if we had truly felt threatened, I would have had Odin use the facility's built-in defense mechanisms, which are under his control. But luckily for Frances and for us, Odin was able to determine from the type of approaching craft and pilot that they were not a threat. Odin did, however, still interfere with Frances's communications until he could confirm that my family was ready to reveal its existence to the outside world again, which is why you had trouble reaching her at first. But we eventually ordered Odin to restore her ability to communicate from our facility."

"You mentioned a new atmosphere, Robert," Thomas continued. "What do you know about it?"

"When it first developed at our location," Robert began,

"we referred to it as proto-atmosphere. It was remarkably similar to what scientists once thought Earth's early atmosphere was like. As we cleared a larger area, the new atmosphere began changing and becoming closer to what Earth's atmosphere was like during the twenty-first century. Then, with Valhalla's sensors cleared, Odin computed that a combination of chemicals from the mixture from the comet, from the propellants of the thrusters, and from Lunar Sister's soil was allowing the atmosphere to expand and to alter the mixture over an ever-growing area. Within time, I believe there will be an atmosphere surrounding the entire moon. We also determined that the comet had somehow influenced the rotation of the moon, causing gravity to at least double from one-sixth of Earth's gravity to one-third of Earth's gravity. I'm hoping you might be able to confirm that for us?" Robert inquired.

"Your findings seem close to ours," Thomas confirmed. "But we're still studying this unusual event and the gravitational changes. All crafts here have had to make adjustments, and at first, we couldn't figure out why. But we eventually began to suspect the same as you, that the moon's gravity has changed. Maybe we can work together on this and come up with the most plausible answer."

"Yes, Father," Frances agreed. "But for now, let's be good hosts and offer them something to eat and drink?" Frances knew her father well and knew that if she didn't pause him, he might continue making conversation forever. "The MacMurchaids can, I'm sure, fill us in more afterward. For example, they mentioned that they even have animals in hibernation at Valhalla. And a garden."

"Okay, first we eat," Thomas agreed. "But then, I want to learn more. I also want to get to know all of you better personally. As you're famous historical figures and our ancestors, we already know quite a bit about you. But it's an entirely different thing to have the opportunity to really know you."

Frances and Thomas led the MacMurchaid family into a room that was designated for dining and was definitely more comfortable than the dining area at Valhalla. Frances then asked everyone what they would like to eat. Robert spoke up, saying, "I'm sure we'll be more than happy with whatever you offer us. We don't want to impose on your hospitality. Also, since we're newly awakened to this century, I'm not sure we even know what food is like now. Before our mission began, we saw conceptualized depictions of future foods through television and movies. But I'm hoping whatever exists now is even better than we could have imagined."

Thomas looked at the MacMurchaid children and said, "Don't worry, kids. We aren't going to plop pills in front of you with some drink to wash them down. Nor are we going to give you bland food with no taste or seasoning. We're better prepared than that. Plus, there are some traditional family dishes that were passed down to us and we still make today. You might recognize them." He paused, then said, "For example, chocolate dumplings. Does that sound good? What better way to feel at home than that?" Thomas could see the delight in the children's faces, and he noticed slight grins on Robert and Denise's faces.

While they ate chocolate dumplings, the MacMurchaids continued to chat with their hosts about what their lives were like before their mission. Then, after everyone had finished eating and everything was cleared from the table, Thomas said, "Before we sat down to eat, I recall Frances mentioning something about a garden and animals. Can you tell me more?"

As he always did, Robert took the lead explaining. "The garden was automatically planted at Valhalla before Odin awakened me. Its purpose was to provide us with a means of oxygen in case something went wrong with Valhalla's air filtration system. But it was also planted to provide us and the animals with food. The soil the garden is planted in is a mixture of lunar soil and soil brought from Earth prior to our arrival. As for water, since they could only bring a limited amount to store at Valhalla, they decided to gather some of the ice that had been discovered at the lunar south pole. The ice was then stored deep underground at Valhalla to keep it frozen. Once it was needed, it could be melted and sent through a filtration system to ensure it was safe to use." Robert still found it funny how he could tap into so much information he had learned while not even awake.

Robert continued his explanation. "As for the animals, they were placed into Loki's Breath back on Earth, at young ages, and then transported to Valhalla already in a state of hibernation. This was part of the overall grand experiment, which involved seeing if the animals could be trained while under Loki's Breath and seeing if they might be easier to manage once awakened. By the way, we have not awakened any of the animals yet. Previously unbeknownst to us, they even brought our family pets here from Earth to give us comfort if we ever ended up stranded here, as we are now."

"What you've told us so far is fascinating," Thomas responded. "Is there anything more you'd like to share at this time, Robert?"

"Well, again, we've noticed that gravity has increased some since the comet passed by. We suspect that the comet has affected the moon's core, increased lunar rotation, or possibly a combination of both. And while we've been here with you, our two atmospheres have continued closing in on each other and will soon meet. So, we better monitor how they interact with each other," Robert suggested.

"Are you guessing about all of this?" Thomas inquired. "Or do you have some sort of data or observations to back it up?"

Kris jumped in to help explain. "It appears that a by-product of us being in pseudo-death and Odin constantly feeding us data over hundreds of years is that my family and I now have some sort of psychic link to Odin, and we're now in constant communication with him, even while we're here with you. Another by-product of being under Loki's Breath so long is that any physical abnormalities that were previously present in our bodies now seem to be gone. Before our mission, it was explained to us that scientists noticed these kinds of things on a smaller scale during their early experiments with the gas. But it wasn't fully understood at that point. And we still don't fully understand it now. We're still getting used to it. But long story short, we're not guessing. This information comes from Odin."

Thomas and Frances looked on in amazement. Robert told them, "Kris is our medical officer. Since his interest before our mission was to become a doctor, they trained him for it while he was under Loki's Breath and updated his training as new medical advancements were made over the years. We've each received centuries of training for our respective interests."

"We'll have much more to talk about in the future," Thomas said. "For now, we'll keep the existence of your family a secret. We want you to be comfortable with and prepared for other people finding out about your existence. And we'll continue monitoring the two atmospheres from the different sides of the moon and see what happens when they meet. Will their conjoining be peaceful, or will it create some sort of calamity? I guess we'll just have to wait and see."

"We'll know soon," Denise informed him. "Odin is now telling us that the two atmospheres are about to make contact at the western lunar terminus boundary between daylight and darkness."

Chapter 20

Rain on the Moon

F RANCES LED EVERYONE to a room with multiple monitors in it. Thomas pulled up sensor readings and satellite views from the area of the moon that the two atmospheres were approaching. The two masses were growing closer. And within a short time, they met. "According to our sensor readings, the atmospheres have met and appear to be mixing," Frances informed everyone as she continued to watch the monitors.

"The satellite sensor isn't picking up many changes yet, though," Thomas added from looking at the monitor he was reading.

"According to what Odin is sending us," Tony jumped in, "the two atmospheres are mixing and are creating chemical reactions due to the variations in each mass's chemical composition."

Thomas inquired, "Does it appear to anyone else that the lunar surface is getting darker?"

Everyone looked at Thomas's monitor, and Tony was the

first to answer. "Odin states that there appears to be precipitation falling from the area where the atmospheres are mixing, and the precipitation is spreading as the two masses continue to combine over a larger area."

"Our sensors are not set up for reading moisture on the moon, so how is it that Odin is able to detect precipitation?" Frances asked.

Robert explained, "At Valhalla, we still have radar equipment from the twenty-first century. The equipment was not previously modified to lunar conditions the way equipment would be today. So, the old radar still has Doppler capabilities. That's why Odin can detect precipitation. Can your sensors detect the composition of the precipitation, though?"

Frances responded, "They should be able to." After a pause, she continued. "The composition appears to be oxygen hydride with very minor impurities in each drop. Water or rain is falling to the lunar surface for the first time in human history!" Frances exclaimed.

"I presume from our earlier conversation that there are other people on the moon. Maybe you should alert them?" Denise suggested. "I'm not sure they'll believe you, though!" she added.

Picking up on Denise's point, Robert suggested, "You might also want to tell them that due to the increased gravity, they'll have to make some adjustments. Also, since they proved back in the twenty-first century that bacteria and other things can survive meteor impacts on Earth or lay dormant for long periods under extremely cold conditions, I would think that all ground samples and new atmospheric samples should be monitored down to the microscopic level for possible new lifeforms."

Thomas sat contemplating Denise and Robert's suggestions for a few minutes. "I'll make your suggestions known. I don't know how the suggestions will be received by others, but to me, what you've said makes sense and is logical." With that, Thomas and Frances went about putting out alerts to different facilities on the moon. They included data with the alerts, including coordinates where the precipitation was so that those who received the alerts could verify for themselves what was happening.

At the same time, the MacMurchaids continued paying attention to what they were receiving from Odin. The precipitation phenomenon was still increasing in size and was spreading out in all directions. Odin kept the family informed as to what percentage of Lunar Sister's surface was being covered by the precipitation. He informed them that the sensors indicated that at the center of the phenomenon, the precipitation was ceasing but had been able to soak into Lunar Sister's soil in varying depths. Odin's computations on the existing data so far suggested that the precipitation might last thirty-six to forty-nine hours. Sensors also indicated that, in the area where the precipitation had stopped, the temperature was beginning to fluctuate.

The MacMurchaids passed the information from Odin on to the Murchisons so that Thomas and Frances could compare it to the data being reported to them from various facilities and sensors on the moon. Though their sensors had now been adjusted to account for the precipitation, they were still having problems fully detecting it. But like Odin's readings, their sensors did show that the temperature in the area where the precipitation had dissipated was varying.

Thomas and Frances were receiving information from people observing the precipitation from all over the moon. People closer to the phenomenon shared both their sensor readings and what they could visually observe with the naked eye, while those further away shared only their sensor readings. Adding this information to the Murchison's computer helped them create a simulated prediction model as to the course of the precipitation. From this model, the Murchisons and MacMurchaids could see whether Odin's prediction as to the duration of the precipitation was correct.

Communications were now even coming in from observatories on Earth, saying that they noticed something strange happening on the moon. People on Earth could not make out much with the naked eye, but they could see something was different on the moon, and it worried them. To those at the observatories, it looked like a weather front was moving lunar west to lunar east and that a secondary, much smaller, front was moving from lunar east to lunar west. The Murchisons and MacMurchaids were too involved in their own observations to respond to questions from Earth. But others on the moon who were not so tied up fed their data to Earth.

Before long, word had spread on Earth that there was rain on the moon. The news then quickly traveled to outposts throughout the solar system before the phenomenon had finally engulfed the entire moon. Then, the precipitation ceased. As the atmosphere on the moon stabilized, it suddenly took on a blue hue similar to that of Earth's sky.

With the precipitation stopped, both the Murchisons and Odin were able to stop charting the precipitation and start analyzing the related data they had received. The moon did now have an atmosphere, but it was a much thinner atmosphere than that of Earth, and it was too early to see if the new atmosphere would have weather patterns. And with the moon's increased gravity and increased rotation, temperatures around the moon were stabilizing and were more moderate than previously recorded. The moon's new temperatures were not similar to Earth's, but they were no longer the extreme range they had previously been between the light and dark. All of this was completely new to everyone, and all they could do was wait and see what would happen next.

Both the MacMurchaids and the Murchisons decided to take a rest since they had been acting as central data control throughout the precipitation event and had worked throughout the duration of the event. The Murchisons knew they would soon have to start answering questions from people about their involvement in detecting and monitoring the precipitation. Thomas said to Robert, "I appreciate your family's help during this thing. I know I'll have a lot of questions to answer from people, but I'll do my best to keep your family out of it. But I worry that someone might have figured out that Frances and I were receiving help, and that will raise other questions."

Robert looked at his tired family, and each of them nodded toward him. He then told Thomas, "You're family. And family takes care of family. We know we can't hide forever, nor do we want to. We also know that, sooner or later, others will find

Valhalla. We know these things and are ready to help you answer the questions. We'll stand by you and Frances."

Thomas smiled and said, "Thank you. Thank you all, my family."

Chapter 21

The Surprise Announcement

A T THE REQUEST of the other inhabitants of the moon, Colonel Thomas Murchison and Lieutenant Frances Murchison agreed to conduct an interview with them at Lunar Observatory within twenty-four hours after the precipitation event ended. The Murchisons arrived there along with the MacMurchaids well ahead of schedule so that they could make sure the MacMurchaids were hidden before others showed up. The MacMurchaid and Murchison families had already discussed and decided how and when the MacMurchaids would be introduced to everyone else.

First, Thomas and Frances would share most of the information they had about how the new atmosphere had come into being. They would then introduce those who had helped them collect and interpret the data—the MacMurchaid family. The families knew that once the MacMurchaids were introduced, all questions would shift from being about the atmosphere to being about the MacMurchaids. So, timing was important so that everything could be properly addressed. While awaiting the time of the interview, the two families again went over the details and sequence of the events leading to the new atmosphere and the precipitation.

When the time for the interview arrived, Thomas went to a podium and gave a statement. "Thank you all for being here," he began. "As you already know, this all began when a comet passed close to the moon and Earth. Dust from the comet's tail covered the moon but burned up in Earth's atmosphere. The dust was a mixture of frozen chemicals, which caused a chemical reaction. The reaction created a proto-atmosphere similar to early Earth's atmosphere. Since the side of the moon facing away from the sun is under extremely cold temperatures, we thought we wouldn't have to deal with the dust on that side of the moon for quite some time—not until the moon's rotation brought the dust on the dark side into the sunlight."

Thomas paused and took a sip of water, then continued. "Interestingly, however, satellites eventually picked up a similar proto-atmosphere developing on the dark side of the moon. My daughter, Lieutenant Frances Murchison, and I decided that she would take her shuttle to the coordinates of this new event to try to determine what caused it. Sensors on her shuttle indicated that the new proto-atmosphere on the dark side of the moon was slightly different than the one on the lit side. Her investigations led her to discover a previously-unknown facility on the dark side of the moon.

"At the facility Frances discovered, she met a group of people who were already there and studying the new proto-atmosphere. They agreed to help us with our investigation into the proto-atmospheres. With their assistance, we were able to

171

gather even more data and thus to send out alerts to the rest of the moon's inhabitants as to the changes that happened when the two proto-atmospheres—the one from the dark side and the one from the lit side—met and combined. Those changes were that the combined chemistry of the two proto-atmospheres produced water that fell to the lunar surface as rain and spread over the entire moon.

"The new combined atmosphere has since stabilized and has also stabilized the temperatures between the light and dark sides of the moon. Looking up from the moon, we now have a bluish sky over us. We'll continue to monitor the new atmosphere to make sure it remains stable. All these events, combined, are why the moon now looks different to people observing it from Earth. On a related note, it appears that the comet's dust that burned up in Earth's atmosphere caused the hole in the ozone layer to shrink. I will now take questions," Thomas said, certain that he already knew what the first question would be.

"Colonel Murchison," someone in the crowded room spoke up, "who were the people from the dark side of the moon who assisted you?"

"I'm glad you asked," Thomas responded. He signaled Frances to bring the MacMurchaids out. "The answer I'm about to give you will be hard for you to believe and will come as a shock to all humans. These people are my ancestors." Thomas's arm swung to guide people's eyes to the door at the end of the stage. "They are . . . the MacMurchaids!"

There was an audible gasp from the crowd because many people remembered the history of the MacMurchaids dying when the space station was destroyed—an event that was still taught to present-day humans. They had also seen photos of the MacMurchaids, so they knew it was really them. Thomas continued by saying, "I know how everyone must feel right now because I felt the same way when I met the MacMurchaids a short while ago, after my daughter brought them to our home from the facility they've been at for over 455 years. I will now let Major Robert E. MacMurchaid give a brief statement. So, please hold all questions for now."

There was a murmur in the crowd as Robert approached the podium and began speaking. "Thank you, Colonel," he said as the two men smiled at each other. Robert then continued. "I know this is a surprise for all of you. It's a surprise for us to be here as well. So, please let me explain how we came to be here . . ." Robert went on to recount the same story he had told the Murchisons, from arriving at Valhalla and being put into pseudo-death, to being woken by Odin due to the comet, to meeting Frances. He then finished by saying, "The original objective of our mission was to help all of Earth's people by paving the way for entire families to join in space exploration and travel, and so it is extremely fitting that the person to discover us at Valhalla happened to be one of our descendants—a family member. I would now be happy to take questions."

"Major!" someone called out to him from the crowd. "What are your family's plans now?"

Robert responded, "We haven't had time to think about our future plans yet. We've been too focused on the events related to the comet."

Another person asked, "Well, now that you're thinking

about it, do you think you might return to Earth?"

Robert responded, "I'm sure we'll return to Earth for visits. But the Earth you all know is not the same Earth we knew—the one we left behind. I do know that many of our belongings were stored there, in an underground facility, and we would certainly like to locate them. But to find them, we'll likely have to study the Earth's physical changes that have occurred over the last 455 years. We would also like to meet the people of Earth and other descendants of ours. We'll just take each day as it comes and try to enjoy it all."

Thomas, not wanting the MacMurchaids to be bombarded with too many questions, stepped in and said, "That's all for now. As the Major—my ancestor—said, his whole family worked hard through this recent event. They didn't sleep until we were sure everything was stabilized and there wasn't any danger to anyone. We're all tired and would like to rest before we take the next steps, which, as you point out, might include a trip to Earth. Thank you all for your time."

The MacMurchaids and Murchisons all exited through the door they had entered through. They got back onto Frances's shuttle. And they headed back to Valhalla so that Thomas and Frances could have a full tour.

Chapter 22

Return to Earth

AFTER THE MURCHISONS returned the MacMurchaids to Valhalla and finished their tour of the facility, they left. The MacMurchaids settled in for a much-needed period of rest after their newfound family members left. They kept going over data that was coming in concerning the new lunar atmosphere. And they knew they would have to meet with the public again at some point. But for now, they mostly tried to relax.

The MacMurchaids decided to hold off on waking the animals until they were sure they had everything they would need on hand to properly take care of them, including the time to do so. If they woke them now, they wouldn't have time to care for them since they were considering visiting Earth. They knew that once they woke the animals, their family would basically be homesteading on the moon and likely unable to all leave at once. And they weren't yet sure if that was the life they wanted going forward.

Robert and Denise knew that the Murchisons would not reveal the location of Valhalla to anyone. But they figured that people would now be searching for it and that it was only a matter of time before someone else discovered it. The family members had to make decisions about their future. Would their renewed fame ever allow them to be themselves, or would they be forever inundated with requests for interviews and appearances? From what they had been told, there were now outposts throughout the solar system and even contact made with beings beyond the solar system. As intriguing as it was to the Mac-Murchaids to visit other worlds, they knew that now was not the time.

After a few days alone together without any outside contact—except from Thomas and Frances—and without needing to be constantly poring over data, the MacMurchaids were beginning to fall into a regular routine around their new home at Valhalla. And they enjoyed the routine, as well as their communications with Odin. Odin had begun to show signs of communicating more fluidly and less robotically. It almost felt to the MacMurchaids as though he were becoming a member of their family.

Eventually, Frances contacted Robert to let him know that there were descendants of the MacMurchaids on Earth who would like to meet their family. She warned them, however, that the media of the present was in many ways still like the media they knew from the past and might hound them if they visited Earth. The MacMurchaids were surprised to learn that their descendants apparently lived close to where the Heavener Runestone used to be. But no one was sure whether the stone had survived the war and, if it had, whether it was still located where it used to be.

Heavener, Oklahoma was near Poteau, Oklahoma, where Cavanal Hill was. That's where Geoff Pitts had told the Mac-Murchaids their possessions were being stored, deep underneath the hill. With their descendants there, their belongings potentially still there, and it being their old home state, it started to make more and more sense to the MacMurchaids to visit Oklahoma, even if it meant potentially being overwhelmed by the media. With all that had happened during the war and with the shifts in Earth's crust, they wondered if they would even be able to locate Cavanal Hill. And if they did, would their things still be buried in storage there?

Odin had been monitoring the family's thoughts and decided to communicate with them. "There is a device here that can locate the signal from the buried vault and the passage used to reach it," Odin informed Robert. Robert was glad to hear this and was impressed with how smooth Odin's communication now was. Odin gave Robert the location of the device within Valhalla. Once Robert had located it, he gathered his entire family together to communicate with the Murchisons.

When the Murchisons appeared on a monitor in front of the family, Robert said, "My family would like to visit our descendants on Earth. But we would like to visit with them privately. No media."

Thomas replied, "I can understand and respect that. It will be a challenge pulling that off, though. Word of your existence has already spread throughout the solar system. You're among the most famous faces on Earth right now."

"Yes. But we've been going through some old communications from Congressmen Pitts," Robert informed Thomas. "And it turns out that locating our possessions that were stored prior to our mission should be easier than we thought. So, we have some added incentive to go, even with the risks involved."

Thomas said, "Tell me more about this vault where your possessions are stored. I don't understand."

Robert said, "In preparing for our mission, arrangements were made for a vault to be created in a hill in the city of Poteau, Oklahoma. The hill would have been west of where we lived, but with Earth's crust having shifted, it would now be located east of where our house used to be. The vault was constructed from an old coal strip pit, which created a sloping passageway down, ending in a chamber at the bottom, which is where the vault was placed.

"The government knew that we would soon become some of the most famous people on Earth, and so they moved our possessions from our home to the vault. The entrance to the passageway leading to the vault was disguised to look like part of the hill and the surrounding area. My family very well might be the only people left who knew of its existence. And it would be fun to retrieve our possessions, which include a genealogy chart that Denise put together. Do you think you can help us locate the vault, or do you know someone trusted who can?" Robert asked.

Thomas replied, "I can understand your desire to retrieve your possessions. And with your renewed fame, I'm sure they've become incredibly valuable and need to be protected. But how sure are you that the vault is even intact and can be accessed? It's been centuries since it was sealed."

Robert said, "I'm not sure about accessibility. But the vault was made of a special alloy to purposefully allow slow corrosion. And the vault, the chamber, and the passageway were supposedly filled with an inert gas that would also slow or stop any deterioration. So, to complicate matters, if we do find the door to the passageway, we would have to flush out the gas. I'm not too certain that any of this can be accomplished. But we're willing to try if it means we might access some sort of reminder of what life used to be like for us—even a small reminder."

Thomas pondered things for a minute, then said, "I'll see what I can arrange. Since the population in that area is still sparse, we might be able to do this without any media showing up. I'll try to set something up for you to search for the vault prior to meeting with your relatives."

Robert thanked Thomas and said he would wait to hear more from him. And the entire MacMurchaid family said goodbye. A couple of days later, Thomas called again and confirmed that he had made arrangements for the MacMurchaids to make a secret visit to Earth and that he and Frances would be joining them during the visit.

* * *

When the time came, the MacMurchaids and Murchisons traveled to Earth, located what was left of what had been known as Cavanal Hill, and powered up the device Odin had given them so that they could locate the entrance to the passageway that would lead them to their vault. In no time, the device led them to where the entrance *should* have been. But the MacMurchaids were dismayed to discover that the natural surroundings had jumbled everything around the entrance together over time.

Both families cleared brush, stones, and other debris away until, finally, Kris discovered what appeared to be a metal door. The families excitedly cleared out the edges of the door and further discovered a well-hidden control box attached to it. They tried powering up the box, but nothing happened. Expecting this, they had brought with them a power supply, which they adapted to match the box's voltage and amperage until finally, the box lit up.

Troy said, "Okay, people, step back. If the gas has escaped, you won't want to breathe it in when this door opens." He then used the device they had to send a signal to the box, causing the door to unseal and slightly open. Troy took a deep breath, held it in, and pulled open the door.

Using sensors they had brought with them, the families checked the air quality at the door's entrance, then a little ways inside it. Frances said, "Well, if there was truly gas in here, then it appears it must have leaked out quite a long time ago. The air here is completely breathable, though a little stale!"

"Okay, everyone," Robert took over. "From here on down, we need to use our breathing apparatuses. So, before entering this door, make sure yours is working and keep an eye on each other for any signs of struggling to breathe."

Both families slowly and cautiously descended the sloping passageway until they reached a second door. After opening it, checking the air quality on the other side, and confirming the air was okay, they continued until they reached a third door. This time, when they opened the door, they detected gas. But the gas wasn't as potent as it would have been when it was first placed there over 455 years earlier. With their breathing apparatuses, the families were able to continue unharmed. After descending a short way further, they finally reached the vault.

Robert and Thomas walked around the vault, checking for any damage. But all they found were some dents where they figured large rocks must have fallen from the roof of the chamber they were in. The floor was littered with rocks that would not have been there when the chamber was created. Using the device they had brought with them, Troy signaled the vault, and the vault opened. The gas inside the vault was stronger than the gas outside it, but it, too, was weaker than it originally would have been.

Once the door to the vault was fully open, it revealed its contents: several wrapped and sealed containers as well as the MacMurchaids' old furniture. The MacMurchaids did not bother with the furniture. But, working in teams, the families were able to carry the containers to the surface where the shuttlecraft they had all arrived on was parked nearby. Once everything they wanted was emptied out of the vault and loaded onto the craft, Troy resealed the vault and then resealed each passageway door behind the families as they left. When they shut the final door—between the passageway and the outside world—they covered it and the control box as best they could with dirt, rocks, and branches.

Everyone boarded the craft, and they departed the area to a preselected location where another craft was waiting. The MacMurchaids boarded the second craft while Thomas and Frances took the first craft back to the Murchisons' facility on the moon. Although the family the MacMurchaids were scheduled to visit with were also Thomas and Frances's relatives, the Murchisons had already visited with them many times before and decided to let them have the MacMurchaids all to themselves this time. On board their shuttle, the MacMurchaids changed clothes and stored their dirty clothes in a locker. They did not want to raise suspicions as to what they had been up to.

After the MacMurchaids took off in their shuttle, they began on a low flight path before eventually climbing to a higher one. They then made a few maneuvers designed to make it look to anyone who might be monitoring their craft like they had just arrived from the moon. After a short trip, they landed safely outside their descendants' home, and the family that lived there hurriedly came out to greet the MacMurchaids. Robert said to his family, "Denise, kids, these are the Hunters: our descendants."

One of the Hunters, an older man, approached Denise and said, "I'm Phil. And this is my wife, Rhonda. And these are our two children, Connie and Dustin. Rhonda is a descendant of Robert's brother." Phil held out his hand to shake Denise's, but she instead hugged him. She then proceeded to hug each of the other members of the Hunter family.

The rest of the Hunters and MacMurchaids then made individual introductions and greeted each other as well. The Hunters invited the MacMurchaids in, but Robert declined on behalf of their family, saying, "That's all right. We wouldn't want to be a bother. Besides, it's so nice outside today, and we haven't been able to enjoy Earth like this in over 455 years, so maybe we could sit out here and talk a while?" Feeling the warmth of the sun, Robert thought back to the unusually hot day when Congressman Geoff Pitts arrived at the MacMurchaid home to announce their selection for the Valhalla mission.

Everyone agreed to staying outside. The MacMurchaid children acted just like they had before their mission had begun, playing with their distant cousins while the adults talked. After over an hour of conversation and play, an Earth vehicle suddenly appeared. Phil had an uneasy feeling that this was a member of the media. And he was correct.

"Mr. MacMurchaid! Could I get an interview?!" a man called from the window of the vehicle before even exiting it. Phil started to get up to shoo the man away, but Robert waved him off.

Robert said, "I'll handle this, Phil. Please continue enjoying yourselves and the company of my family." He then wandered over to the reporter and told the man, "My family is here to have a quiet and peaceful time with relatives. As long as you don't attempt to bother any of them, I'll speak with you. Do you understand?"

The reporter could see Robert's stern look and knew that he could be in for the scoop of a lifetime as long as he complied. So, he said, "Yes, sir!" He then exited his vehicle, and he and Robert walked further away from the families so they could speak with each other. The reporter turned on a recording device and said, "We heard what you said on the moon to its inhabitants, and we further investigated your story thereafter. So, we somewhat know the history of your family and what really happened during your mission. But the people of Earth would love to learn more than that. Can you give us any further details we might not already know?"

Robert paused for a moment and looked around at his sur-roundings, remembering Oklahoma as it was before his family left. Finally, he said, "Prior to leaving Earth, my family lived a simple life. We were considered low-income, but we were far from poor. We did not have a lot, but we had each other. Denise and I tried to raise our children with the values with which we were raised. The main thing to us is that family is important above all else. Family is more important than money or materi-al things.

"Denise and I raised our children with love, but they still had rules to follow, like Denise and I did growing up. We taught them to remember their family history. Our children were told that not all of our ethnic ancestors were treated well or equally and that they were sometimes treated quite poorly. And we raised them to see only one race: the *human* race. There might be many different ethnicities, but the human race is the only race as far as the MacMurchaids are concerned.

"We also raised our children on the value that if you're go-ing to do a job, then do your best while doing it. If you give someone your word that you're going to do something, then you keep that word and do not break it. The children knew I had been in the Air Force and that I was honorably discharged due to family problems. I tried to reenlist in another branch of service, but by then, I had a family, and they said I had too many dependents to enlist. They said that if I would divorce Denise and sign the children over to her, then I could reenlist, and then I could later remarry here. But I declined to do so. As much as I wanted to serve my country, my family was more important, and I chose my family over the military.

"We have taken our children to many special events, have taken them on camping trips where we had to make our own shelter and bedding, and taught them as much as we could about nature. Together, as a family, we have learned more things outside of school than we ever did *in* school. History was one subject we particularly enjoyed. So, to make an already long story shorter, we're a family that lives, learns, and teaches about the importance of family." Robert paused there, and he then finished by saying, "I'm sure we'll meet again in the future. But for now, if you don't mind, I would like to get back to my family."

The reporter kept his word to be respectful, turned off his recording device, and said to Robert, "Thank you for your time. And I hope you enjoy your remaining time here on Earth." The man returned to his Earth vehicle, got in, and left. As for Robert, he returned to his family and descendants.

When the children from both families started showing signs of tiredness, the adults decided it was time for the Mac-Murchaids and Hunters to part ways. Hugs were given all around, and goodbyes were said. The MacMurchaids loaded into their shuttlecraft, and the Hunters gathered on the porch of their house to wave goodbye. As the shuttle lifted into the air, the MacMurchaids glanced around at the scenery, taking in their last up-close looks at Earth. Then, their shuttle headed back toward the moon and toward their new home at Valhalla. Robert set the shuttle's controls to auto so that it could safely fly them there. The entire family relaxed, and soon, everyone was asleep.

Chapter 23

Heroes' Welcome

WHEN THE MACMURCHAIDS had awoken from their naps, they were nearing the moon and had received a message from Frances Murchison. The message asked the MacMurchaids to meet the Murchisons at the Lunar Observatory before returning to Valhalla. Frances's reasoning was that her mother, Lorene Murchison, had returned a week early from her trip to the Trans-Mars Observatory. Having just returned, she was debriefing at the Lunar Observatory and hoped to meet the MacMurchaids there. Although the Mac-Murchaids were still tired and looking forward to returning home to Valhalla, they reluctantly agreed to stop at the Lunar Observatory on the way.

Once the MacMurchaids' shuttle had landed on the Lunar Observatory platform, they disembarked and saw a woman standing near the observatory's entrance. She was with Thomas and Frances, and so they assumed this must be Lorene. She confirmed it a moment later when she approached Robert, held out her hand, and said, "Hello, I'm Lorene Murchison." She shook Robert's hand and then proceeded to give everyone a hug and a kiss on the cheek.

When Lorene had finished greeting everyone, she said, "I've heard so much about your family. And I've watched a number of news clips about you since you recently resurfaced. I'm sure Thomas and Frances have already welcomed you into our family since we are, in fact, all family. Come on inside where we can get to know each other better. I'm having trouble adjusting to this new atmosphere!"

After everyone had entered the observatory, they walked down a long hallway that ended in the observatory's main chamber. Once there, the MacMurchaids noticed it was incredibly dark inside. Suddenly, the lights flicked on, and a large group of people shouted, "SURPRIIIIISE!"

The MacMurchaids were stunned. Seeing the looks on their faces, Lorene quickly explained, "These people are lunar inhabitants who wanted to welcome you 'back from the dead,' so to speak, and into the twenty-fifth century. They also wanted to thank you for your help during the recent post-comet events. They consider you heroes. I know you must be tired and want to get home. But I hope you'll please enjoy yourselves for a bit and meet some of your fellow lunar inhabitants?"

People were already lining up to greet the MacMurchaids. One by one, the MacMurchaids shook hands with each person in the room. People were saying things to them like, "Welcome back," Thank you," "Glad you're here," and "Hoping to see more of you." Once the MacMurchaids had shaken hands with the last person, everyone was given plates of cake and containers of punch. The MacMurchaids did their best to enjoy themselves despite the people crowding around them and taking photos and the constant conversation. Even before their Valhalla mission, they had not been through anything like this.

Eventually, the MacMurchaids gravitated back to the Murchisons, and the two families began talking amongst themselves with an occasional interruption from a well-wisher. Lorene asked, "Are you all enjoying yourselves? Don't try to hogwash it by being polite. You can tell me the truth."

Kris hesitatingly answered on behalf of his entire family. "We aren't used to this kind of thing. Even before we left Earth for our mission and were starting to gain some degree of fame, we never experienced anything like this. We're simple people, and we feel kind of out of place in this environment. We've never talked to so many people before, let alone been around so many people before!

Lorene said, "Thank you for being honest, young man. To tell you the truth, I don't like big things like this either. The biggest event I feel comfortable at is a family get-together. But this was not my idea. After your interview about the post-comet events and Robert's more recent interview with the reporter in Oklahoma, your family is the talk of the solar system."

The gala continued for what seemed to the MacMurchaids like forever. But people began slowly streaming out, and eventually, the MacMurchaids and Murchisons were the only ones left. At that point, Thomas turned to the MacMurchaids and said, "Thank you all for doing this. Why don't we accompany you to Valhalla to help you unload the things you collected from the vault? And you can then relax in peace."

Robert agreed to Thomas's offer of help. The MacMurchaids and Murchisons returned to their respective shuttles, buckled in, and departed for Valhalla. Valhalla already felt like home to the MacMurchaids, and they were looking forward to returning there with their belongings from their Earth home.

Chapter 24

Home to Valhalla

THE MACMURCHAIDS AND MURCHISONS each flew their shuttles in different directions, turned off their transponders, and turned off as many outer lights as they safely could. Their flights would be done completely by onboard navigational computer assistance. That would help them evade detection from anyone who might be attempting to follow the families and determine Valhalla's location.

Once the shuttles had converged again near the entrance to Valhalla, Robert communicated with Odin to let him know there would be two shuttles entering. Odin opened the doors, and the Murchison's shuttle entered first, followed by the MacMurchaid's shuttle. Once both shuttles were parked, everyone disembarked. The MacMurchaids were relieved to be home.

Robert suggested, "For now, let's leave everything on the shuttle and give Lorene a full tour of Valhalla. Denise, will you and the children escort the Murchisons on the tour while Odin and I work out the details of where the items from the shuttle should be placed?"

Denise nodded her agreement, and she and the children motioned for the Murchisons to follow them. Meanwhile, Robert spoke with Odin, informing him of their shuttle's contents and discussing where everything should go. Once they had finalized their plans, Robert headed to the kitchen and fixed everyone a meal and something to drink. He knew the tour would take quite a while since the Valhalla facility was large and there would likely be a lot of conversation and questions along the way.

Just as Robert was finishing setting everything on the table in the dining area, the tour party returned. Lorene looked at the spread on the table and said, "My, my . . . a man who can cook, set a table, and make sure everything is in place. Denise, you're lucky to have such a man!"

Denise answered, saying, "Even back on Earth, Robert was like this. He was raised by his parents and grandparents to do almost anything. We've done our best to see that our children are raised the same way. It's part of why our family was selected for the Valhalla mission to begin with."

Lorene said, "Well, you're a special family even during this age. Many things are now done by robotics, so children don't learn the same work ethic they used to—at least, not until they're much older."

"Whether there are robotics or not, we still feel it's better to learn how to do things for yourself," Denise informed her. "With the growing popularity of electronics and robotics during our previous life on Earth, too many people were already getting lazy and careless. Some people just didn't seem to care at all about anything anymore. It was an age where a growing number of people were beginning to expect freebies. What they refused to realize was that those so-called freebies were actually being paid for by someone else who worked hard for what they had."

"That's an interesting perspective on life during your time," Lorene commented. "That kind of information sometimes fails to be adequately portrayed when it's passed down through historical recordings and writings to the people of our time. We hope that your family is able to adapt to our time okay and to enjoy it and your new life here."

Robert jumped in, saying, "We've decided to remain awake and not return to our sleep chambers unless absolutely necessary. And though we do have robotic helpers on hand here, we intend to remain a hands-on family. I must admit, however, that we already seem to be becoming quite reliant on Odin. But he now seems like such an individual that it's hard to imagine shutting him out. He's been online for so long and gathered so much information during the years that we were in our sleep chambers that he gained the ability to think for himself. As far as we're concerned, he's the newest member of the MacMurchaid family."

"Thank you for adopting me into your family, Robert," Odin said over the facility's intercom.

"No, thank *you*, Odin," Robert responded. "You're the main reason my family and I are still alive. Family takes care of family, and that is exactly what you've done."

Robert then turned to the Murchisons and said, "We're calling Valhalla our home. And with the items we've brought from the Earth vault, we'll attempt to make it look a little more like our old home. But maybe with not so many messy bedrooms," Robert joked as he gave his children a faux stern look. Everyone laughed, and Robert continued. "I hope we'll get to travel more of the solar system. And while I'm sure we'll visit Earth often, we presently have no plans to ever live there again. That said, among the many things our mission has taught us is that there's no way of knowing for certain what the future will bring. Right, kids?"

Nicole spoke up, saying, "If we're going to travel the solar system, I wonder if, with today's technology, we could give Odin a human-like body with a brain-like system for downloading new information so that he can travel along with us?"

"You mean like the androids we used to see in some science fiction movies and TV shows back on Earth?" Troy asked his sister. "So, he would also be self-aware, think for himself, and make decisions on his own? Is that what you mean?"

Nicole responded, "Yes. That's exactly what I mean. I want him to be with us always. I know that a portion of him will have to remain here, at Valhalla, to make sure things here are okay. But I want him to be with us in physical form when we're traveling."

"We can certainly look into it," Robert assured his daughter. "For now, we're home. We've filled another chapter in the stories of each of our lives. Where we each go from here will be determined by the choices we make along the way as our stories continue—stories that our descendants will learn from."

Everyone enjoyed the meal. When they had finished, the Murchisons left Valhalla for their own home. And the MacMurchaids went to wake their pets.

Author's Note

THE IDEA FOR this book began in the early 1990s. But although I had brief notes and rough drafts, I didn't start actually writing the book until a few years before the turn of the century. Since I grew up during the "space race" between the US and the USSR, I have long been interested in the idea of going to space. As a child, I gave some thought to becoming an astronaut but unfortunately never followed through with it. During my senior year of high school, I delayed enlisted into the United States Air Force and served as a crew member with the Titan II Intercontinental Ballistic Missile during the Cold War. That was the closest I came to my childhood dream since during the Gemini stage of the US's part of the race, it used the Titan II missile as a lift vehicle for the Gemini spacecraft. My interest in space was further strengthened by *Star Trek®*, *2001: A Space Odyssey®*, and similar such stories, television shows, and movies.

My children tended to show interest in the space program as well, mostly during the space shuttle program. My youngest son went in for a minor operation when he was little. That day, there was a shuttle launch while he was waiting to have surgery. When the medical staff started to give him anesthetic gas, he began acting like he was talking to mission control before he went under. And our eldest son and a couple of his classmates decided to do a science fair project based on the space program, so I helped him send for information from the Kennedy Space Center, Johnson Center, and a few other locations. They did not win the science fair, but they did rather well in their age group.

The Heavener Runestone Park, as referenced in this book, is an actual park, and the runestone located there was supposedly created by Norsemen who traveled through Oklahoma. My family lived in Heavener, Oklahoma for a brief time. We visited the runestone a couple of times while there. My wife, Denise, visited it when she was younger, before they had built a building around it. And I had taken my son, Troy, and his cub scout pack there on a field trip. The Heavener Runestone was not the only runestone found in Oklahoma. There were others found in various locations. But this particular stone and its different translations were one of many reasons for using the related names Valhalla, Odin, Loki, and Valkyrie in this book.

The characters in this book are somewhat based on my family and people we have known. Although their ages are based more on what they would have been during the 1990s, the book's plot is set during more modern times. Some locations mentioned in the book might not be widely known but are actual places. And information that helped me write this book came directly from those places or from entities connected to those places.

I feel that we have fallen behind where we should be in

space exploration. Many reasons have arisen to slow our progress, such as costs, politics, wars, and fluctuating interest. Like Werner von Braun, I feel our space pursuits started falling short during the Apollo program. Yes, we made it to the moon and back, but that wasn't the dream. Paraphrasing a line of Maggie McConnell from the movie *Mission to Mars*: our goal is to stand on one celestial body and look to the next. I know that is not exactly how she said it, but the sentiment is the same: once we get to one celestial body, we need to develop technology there to better prepare our way to the next and be safer in the process. We began doing so on the moon but then stopped, for the most part.

The basic idea of this book is that it examines what it would look like if we did complete the next step of developing technology for safer space travel. But the twist is that it is an average, everyday family that is involved in that next step, not just individual trained professionals. After all, isn't there a little bit of explorer in all of us? Aren't we all looking for answers related to subjects, whether they be here on earth or out in space? As I see it, we, the people of Earth, are one race with many ethnic groups, but we are family. To accomplish a positive future, we must all work together as a family and put aside our differences for the greater good.

Though some of the real-world names and places that helped inspire this book have been renamed in the book, many readers will already know or might soon investigate the history of humankind's involvement in space exploration. Let us work together to move toward a better future for all. If this book gets the dream of space exploration to start moving forward in at least one person, then this book is a success. This book is something I am handing down to my children, grandchildren, and hopefully their descendants. But I hope that *anyone* who reads it will find it enjoyable!

From the Publisher

Thank You from the Publisher

Van Rye Publishing, LLC ("VRP") sincerely thanks you for your interest in and purchase of this book.

VRP hopes you will please consider taking a moment to help other readers like you by leaving a rating or review of this book at your favorite online book retailer. Depending on the retailer, you can do so by flipping past the last page of your e-book (to the rating and review page) or by visiting the book's product page (and locating the button for leaving a rating or review).

Thank you!

Resources from the Publisher

Van Rye Publishing, LLC ("VRP") offers the following resources to readers and to writers.

For *readers* who enjoyed this book or found it useful, please consider receiving updates from VRP about new and discounted books like this one. You can do so by following VRP on

Facebook (at www.facebook.com/vanryepub) or Twitter (at www.twitter.com/vanryepub).

For *writers* who enjoyed this book or found it useful, please consider having VRP edit, format, or fully publish your own book manuscript. You can find out more and submit your manuscript at VRP's website (at www.vanryepublishing.com).

Thank you again!

Acknowledgments

T HIS BOOK IS further dedicated to the remembrance of family. I want my family members who passed before this book was completed to always be remembered by my remaining and future family members. But we, as the human race, are really *all* family. So, I also want to dedicate this book to those members of our human family who were explorers and discoverers throughout the told and untold history of the human presence on this planet we call Earth. In making this dedication, I acknowledge the following people who lost their lives in pursuit of mankind's continued exploration of space. Our memory of them and their pursuits is key to our future pursuits.

USA, LT. COL. VIRGIL I. (GUS) GRISSOM, USAF
USA, LT. CDR. ROGER B. CHAFFEE, USN
USA, LT. COL. EDWARD H. WHITE II, USAF
USSR, VLADIMIR KOMAROV
USA, AIRCRAFTMAN 2ND CLASS WILLIAM F.
BARTLEY JR., USAF
USA, AIRMAN 3RD CLASS RICHARD G. HARMAN,
USAF

Acknowledgments

USSR, GREGIY T. DOBROVOLSKY
USSR, VIKTOR I. PATSAYEV
USSR, VLADISLAW N. VOLKOV
USA, FRANCIS R. (DICK) SCOBEE
USA, MICHAIL J. SMITH, USN
USA, RONALD E. MCNAIR
USA, JUDITH A. RESNIK
USA, ELLISON S. ONIZUKA
USA, SHARON CHRISTA MCAULIFFE, TEACHER IN
SPACE PARTICIPANT
USA, GREGORY JARVIS
AND
THOSE WHOSE NAMES DIDN'T MAKE IT INTO THE
HISTORY BOOKS BUT WHO CONTRIBUTED TO THE
CONTINUATION OF EXPLORATION AND DISCOVERY

About the Author

ROBERT E. MURCHISON was born and raised in Muskogee, Oklahoma, with the exception of four years spent living in Columbus, Ohio, while his father was stationed there. His parents raised him with assistance from his maternal grandparents. And with that upbringing, he was taught to appreciate family and history, which are themes that play out in his writing. The main characters in Robert's debut novel, *A Family of Time: A Space Exploration Science Fiction Novel*, are based on his four children and his late wife, who encouraged him to write the book. He and his children are registered members of the Cherokee Nation of Oklahoma. And his children share his appreciation of family, as well as his appreciation of and interest in space and space exploration.

Robert gained his interest in space and space exploration from growing up during the "space race" between the US and USSR, from TV shows and movies related to space and space exploration, and from being a veteran of the United States Air Force, where he served as a launch crew member for the Titan II Intercontinental Ballistic Missile. His other pursuits have included being a substitute teacher, a cub master, and a scoutmaster. And he is currently the historian and an honor guard member for Carnie Welch American Legion Post 27. Robert considers himself a jack of all trades but a master of none. He seeks to continue learning and to continue sharing what he's learned, including via his writing.

www.ingramcontent.com/pod-product-compliance
Lightning Source LLC
Chambersburg PA
CBHW072056170626
46813CB00004B/1379